LOVE

&

GUNPLAY

Love & Gunplay
An Animal novelette

K'WAN

Visit the author website:
www.kwanfoye.com

"Dedicated to #TEAMANIMAL supporters, across the globe. My readers are the best on the planet, hands down! You guys continue to inspire me to reach new heights. We are indeed an unstoppable movement.

--K'wan

PROLOGUE

K-Dawg sat on the porch of his expansive farm house. It rested on two acres of land nestled in a dense area along the coast of Old San Juan Puerto Rico. His lanky frame was slumped in a lawn chair, legs crossed, sipping cognac from a tall glass. They had spilled rivers of blood and burned bridges they'd never be able to cross again on their journey, but K-Dawg didn't give a fuck. It was all or nothing and everybody who wasn't of that thinking would be removed. Staring out at the land he couldn't help but to wonder how he'd gone from a lil project nigga with a chip on his shoulders to a king in his own paradise?

He and his crew had just pulled a caper that was being talked about from the gutters of Puerto Rico to the bathroom stalls of Washington, D.C. Cruz was dead and Poppito was the new boss. All of this was made possible thanks to K-Dawg. It was he and his crew that shifted balance of power in Puerto Rico in Poppito's favor and in return they had been granted a seat at his table. They were all about to be very rich men, but K-Dawg still felt unfulfilled. His plan had been successful, but it wasn't without its unexpected snags.

The low growling of his pit bull Isis, who had been lying at his feet, drew K-Dawg's attention to the path that led from the jungle to farm house. Several figures had emerged from the brush and were making their way up the beach. There were fewer of them returning than he had dispatched but K-Dawg wasn't the least bit surprised. Their mission had been to capture what could not be held and they'd failed, just as he'd expected.

The soldiers were led by Justice. He was a burly, but handsome man who had rock star features, but a street cat's demeanor. He wore his long black hair braided into two ponytails that hung down past his broad shoulders. There was a trail of blood across his brown cheek, just under a thin gash that would likely leave a scar. There was a look in Justice's eyes that K-Dawg hadn't seen in many years. It was hatred. This made K-Dawg smile.

Clutched in Justice's meaty palm was the arm of an attractive Hispanic girl. She had hair the color of a forest fire and eyes of the coldest grey. Justice shoved the girl forward with so much force that she stumbled and K-Dawg had to catch her to keep her from falling on her face. She yanked free of K-Dawg and turned her murderous stare on Justice. He took a step forward as if he wanted hit her but a look from K-Dawg changed his mind.

"I fucked up." Justice finally said after an uncomfortable silence. "I had him cornered until this bitch Sonja stepped in."

Sonja threw her head back and gave a throaty laugh. "The only bitch I see tonight is you, Jus. I'd have thought you'd be happy that I stepped in, because brotherly love wasn't going to save your ass. Have you forgotten so quickly?"

Justice bristled when Sonja called him out. That night, for the first time in their lives, Justice and his baby brother had been on opposite sides of a deadly standoff. In the face of a troupe of armed men Justice had expected Animal to come quietly, but he should've known better. All Animal had was a knife, but it was all he needed to do a considerable amount of damage. The speed with which he moved even surprised his brother and by the time the first shots were fired Animal had already killed two of Justice's men. Justice was hesitant to hurt his brother, but unfortunately Animal had no such reservations. Justice had heard tales of how ruthless his brother was, but it was only when he found himself pinned down with a knife tearing through the soft flesh of his cheek did he realize how accurate the stories had been. Animal acted as if he and Justice hadn't come from the same womb and he was just another nameless meal for the beast that drove him. In the end it had been Sonja's frantic scream that brought Animal back to his senses and saved Justice's life. Watching Animal disappear into a stand of trees Justice knew that the bond they swore would never be broken had been. The last of his family was truly dead to him.

"K-Dawg, I can bring him back," Justice said. "We all know where he's going so all we have to do is send some men to cut him off. I'll go personally to make sure he doesn't get away again."

K-Dawg pondered it for a few seconds. "Yeah, we'll send someone but it won't be a soldier, it'll be a priest. I have a feeling our little love - sick friend is about to open Pandora's Box. When he does, no one short of God will be able to close it." He laughed.

Justice frowned. "K-Dawg, I'm glad you can find humor in this but I don't see what's funny? Animal could fuck up everything that we've got going on."

"Animal can't do shit other than what I allow him to do. No matter what his twisted ass mind tells him, he's still a dog on a leash that I'm holding." K-Dawg approached Sonja, who was staring at him venomously. "Red Sonja," he walked in a short circle around the girl. "It is out of respect for your father that I'm not going to feed your trifling ass to Isis for what you've done."

"Fuck you, K-Dawg. I'm not one of these yes-men who are so afraid of you and your threats. I've gone up against harder cats and they all cried like bitches as I carved them up! You know how I'm built, so do what you do!" Sonja snarled.

K-Dawg laughed. "Indeed, I know just how you're built," he grabbed Sonja by the jaws and leaned in so that they were nose to nose. "Now, let me tell you how I'm built, lil bitch!" He applied pressure. "I have nothing to lose and everything to gain. Every mutha fucka who stands between me and what I want is expendable. That includes your precious father. You thought you were fucking up my plans by setting that rabid dog free, but all you did was speed up the inevitable. Your lil boyfriend and I will see each other again soon enough, this you can count on," he kissed her lips.

Sonja spat in his face. "Good. I hope I'm there to see Animal cut your black heart out!"

K-Dawg's wiped the spit from his face and licked the moisture off his fingers. "There's one thing that I think you're forgetting," he pulled the gun from his waist and shot the soldier standing closest to Sonja. Blood and brains splattered on the side of her face. "I don't have a heart to cut out. Justice," he turned to his best friend, who was the only one who didn't appear to be shocked by what K-Dawg had done, "get somebody to clean this mess up. We got plans to make."

CHAPTER 1

Animal stood on the deck of the cargo ship, huddled in a parka that sported the ship's insignia. It had been drizzling off and on since that morning, but nothing too heavy. Most of the crew was below deck and trying to keep dry, but Animal welcomed the rain splattering on his face. For the past two days he had been held up in his little cabin with only artificial light and stale air. The natural breeze whipping through his hair felt good. In the distance he could see his destination; the Port of Miami. He was getting closer.

Sonja's word had been good. Animal hooked up with her contact who was to smuggle him out of Puerto Rico. He was an old head named Pablo who owned a boat. The tub was beat to hell, but it managed to survive the journey from Puerto Rico to the coast of La Romana in the Dominican Republic. Pablo had a friend who worked on a cargo ship that made runs between some of the islands and the states, so he called in a favor and got Animal a job as a deck hand. The work was slave-like and he had to share his cabin with a family of rats, but he endured for the sake of getting back to Gucci. Once in Miami he was to meet another of Sonja's contacts who would not only get him to New York, but also provide a few *essentials*.

Red Sonja had risked a lot to help him escape, including her own life. If he'd ever doubted whether she truly loved him or not, her selflessness proved that she did. Though he would never admit it, he loved her too, but his heart was already promised to another, so he and Sonja would never be.

As the ship pulled into the port and the crew prepared to unload their cargo, the rain suddenly stopped. Animal took it as a good sign. The air was thick and humid, but at least he wouldn't get any wetter than he already was. Two crewmen rounded the corner and spotted Animal. One turned his eyes to the floor and made hurried steps past Animal, while the other simply nodded. The quiet man who they had picked up in the Dominican Republic had been the topic of quite a few hushed conversations amongst the crew. Animal went about his days doing the work that was required of him, hardly ever speaking and he took his meals in his cabin instead of in the mess hall with the rest of the crew. This didn't make him very popular with the other crew members, but Animal wasn't on the tub to win a popularity contest. He needed to get to Miami.

Securing the backpack that contained what little he owned, Animal picked up a crate and fell in step with two crewmen who were wheeling a flatbed down the gangplank. At the bottom of the ramp he spotted two men in uniforms, carrying assault rifles, inspecting cargo and paperwork of everyone getting off the boat.

As Animal and the crewmen stopped for their cargo to be inspected, one of the officers stared at him. His mouth suddenly became very dry and he began to doubt Sonja's foolproof plan. There was no doubt in Animal's mind that he would go all out if they tried to apprehend them, but he knew he didn't stand a chance. He was so preoccupied trying to spot potential escape routes that he didn't even realize one of the officers were talking to him until he repeated himself in a sterner tone.

"Sak passé?" the dark - skinned officer said to Animal.

Animal tilted his head quizzically. "Huh? I'm sorry I don't understand."

"I said what's happening? Aren't you Haitian, brother?" the officer questioned, studying Animal's features.

"Oh, nah man. I ain't Haitian."

The officer looked at Animal as if he might've been lying. "Funny, you look it. Have a good day, sir." He stepped aside for Animal and the crewmen to pass with their cargo.

Once he was a safe distance from the officers, Animal breathed a sigh of relief. That had been close...too close. He needed to put some distance between him and anyone wearing a uniform. When he was out of sight of the officers he broke away from he crewmen and disappeared between two warehouses. He tossed the box and the parka in the nearest trash can and bid them and the ship good riddance.

Animal looked down at the tattered blue jeans and dingy white t-shirt he had been wearing for the past three days and almost shed a tear. It was a far cry from the rock star he had once been, but that star faded long ago. All that remained was the regret at what might've been and the bitterness of what had become. He was a man who had fallen from grace and landed in exile. It was love that had brought him back and gunplay was the order of business.

"Welcome to Miami, Mr. Collins." The young lady behind the front desk of the Fontainebleau Hotel looked from the handsome brown face on the California issued driver's license, to the man standing in front of her to make sure they were one in the same. "Are you here on business or vacationing?" she made small talk while typing his information into the computer to set up his reservation.

"A bit of both, I gather." Animal replied in an easy drawl. He was now dressed in a black t-shirt and a Miami heat fitted hat pulled tightly over his mop of hair. He had picked shirt and hat up along with a few other pieces at one of the over priced shops on South Beach before he hit the hotel. He hated putting on new clothes without washing his ass, but the raggedy clothes he was wearing drew more stares than the parka would have. While the young lady entered the phony information from the credit card and identification Animal had given her, he casually surveyed the plush hotel lobby, taking mental pictures of every face he laid eyes on. When he turned his attention back to the young lady behind the desk she was giving him a quizzical look.

She was embarrassed that he caught her looking at him and blushed. "I'm sorry, I didn't mean to stare. I just can't help but to feel like I've seen you somewhere before?"

"I doubt it." Animal said, unconsciously tugging at the brim of his fitted.

"Are you sure, because I'm pretty good at remembering faces?" She leaned on her elbows across the desk, showing just enough cleavage to get him to look.

For the first time since he'd been standing there, Animal took stock of the young lady. She was a white girl with a Jersey Shore tan and plastic knockers, with an ass that ass tested the limits of her tan skirt's seams. Whether she grew it or bought it was anyone's guess.

"Nah, this is my first time in Miami so I don't think so." he told her.

"Oh, a virgin, huh?" she flashed her perfectly spaced white teeth. We'll, I'm sure you'll find something to get into or something will find you." She flirted.

"That's what I'm trying to avoid." Animal mumbled under his breath.

"Miami is like Fantasy Island and you can get pretty much anything you want, as long as you're willing to pay for it."

"I'll keep that in mind." Animal he gave her a polite nod and gathered his shopping bags. He could feel her eyes on him as he walked towards the elevator.

"Mr. Collins." She called after him. "If there's anything I can do to make your stay a more pleasant one, just ring the front desk. My name is Jenny and I'll be on duty until midnight."

"Thank you, Jenny. You just might be hearing from me." Animal smiled, flashing a mouth full of gold and diamonds before continuing to the elevator. Pressing his back against the elevator door he took a deep breath. Monkey-fucking the white girl would be just what the doctor ordered considering the amount of stress he was under, but he had to focus on his wants and therefore put his needs on hold.

Jenny assigned Animal to a suite on the seventh floor, which he took as a good sign being that seven was a lucky number. With what he was setting out to do he would need all the luck he could get. Holding the elevator door open, he hesitated for a few seconds before stepping off. He approached his room, which was at the furthest end of the hall, and listened to the door for a minute before sliding his key in the lock.

When he stepped inside the foyer of the suite he was greeted by the low hum of the air conditioner. The air outside had become very humid after the rain, so the light chill sweeping through his room was quite welcome. It was an extravagant suite that was fit for a king, and way more space than he would need, but after what he had been through he deserved to ball for a minute. Besides, in addition to the dummy credit cards Sonja had provided him with, he had an asshole full of cash to play with that he had managed to snatch up before fleeing Puerto Rico. With the play money at his disposal it made it had not to ball just a little bit, especially in Miami.

Animal checked the bathrooms and closets of the suite and only when he was certain that he was alone did he relax. He peeled off the outfit he'd bought on the strip and placed them one of the hotel laundry bags, before heading to the bathroom to wash several days worth of stink off his ass. Turning the shower water on as hot as he could stand it, Animal stepped into the glass stall. Animal welcomed the blazing hot spray of water. He scrubbed his body raw from head to toe, trying to wash away the smell of salt and mold that he had picked up on the boat. It felt good to take an actual shower instead of washing up in sinks as he'd been doing for the past week or so. The scalding water felt good, like a cleansing of not only his body, but his soul and all that it had endured during his exile.

After taking his shower Animal went back into the sleeping area and stretched out naked and wet across the plush bed. The pillow-top mattress seemed to hug him lovingly like he was an angel floating on a stray cloud. He inhaled deeply of the comforter and was greeted by the scent of fabric softener instead of the moldy scent from the tattered blankets on the ship. He closed his eyes and enjoyed the first semblance of peace he'd had since escaping Puerto Rico. His body and soul were weary and he needed to rest but there was still much for him to do in Miami.

Forcing himself into a sitting position, Animal grabbed the bags of clothes he'd purchased and dumped them over the bed. He popped the tags off a pair of blue denim shorts and white I-Zod polo. Sitting on top of a red Nike box were a crisp pair of white Air Force Ones. Once he was dressed he checked himself out in the mirror and nodded in approval at the person who stared back at him. He was looking good and feeling good. The only thing that he needed was a blunt of something sticky to fire up, but since he didn't have that he'd have to settle for the mini-bar. He removed two nips of scotch which he poured into one of the hotel glasses. Sipping his poison, Animal stepped out onto the suite's balcony and observed his surroundings.

The hotel gave Animal a nice view of the beach. He had been to a great many cities during his rap career but this was his first time in Miami and he was impressed. It wasn't so much that the city itself fascinated him, but the energy it gave off. The Miami scene was like the subtle pull of a magnet and he could understand why when some people visited they found themselves reluctant to leave. Maybe one day he would bring Gucci down with him and let her go crazy in the high end stores, but first he needed to get to her. Turning his mind back to business, Animal downed the scotch and prepared to go meet Diamonds.

Animal was feeling good when he reemerged in the hotel lobby. He was fresh, clean and had a nice buzz going on, courtesy of the Fountain Bleau's mini bar. He wasn't drunk, but he had taken enough of the edge off to relax and slipped a little further into himself.

When he passed the front desk, he looked for Jenny but she wasn't at her station. Instead there was a tall light skinned cat with a processed wave manning her post. He was hunched over the desk flirting with two curvaceous chicks that were checking into the hotel. One of the girls caught sight of the chocolate Harlem native floating threw the lobby and zeroed in on him like he was a piece of meat. She tapped her friend and pointed in Animal's direction. They whispered something to each other and shared a giggle. Animal stealing the light skinned dude's shine didn't go over well with him and he didn't bother trying to hide it when he twisted his face up into a scowl. Dude tried to look tough, but Animal could smell the pussy coming off him from across the lobby. To add insult to injury Animal nodded at the two girls and smiled. They responded by motioning for him to come over, but he declined, pointing at his watch to let them know he was pressed for time. Animal knew that if he wanted to, he could've probably gotten both of them to come up to his suite, but he wasn't there for that.

The temperature had dropped a bit as it was approaching nightfall, but it was still very warm. Animal thought he would be able to catch a cab near the hotel but it was easier said than done. One of the valets offered to call one for him, but Animal declined, instead asking for a phone book and a phone he could use. He didn't want anyone to be able to make the connection between the hotel and his destination. He had called several taxi companies but whenever he gave them the address he was going to they refused to take him. He hung up the phone in frustration and tried to brainstorm another mode of transport.

"You need a ride, boss?"

"What?" Animal turned and was confronted with one of the valets. He was a hip looking young cat with a gold tooth in the side of his mouth.

"I didn't mean to eavesdrop, but I overheard you having some trouble getting a taxi." The valet said.

"Yeah, these niggaz act like they scared to go into a black neighborhood." Animal said in frustration.

"Most of them are. I might be able to help you. Where are you trying to go?" the valet asked.

"To this address." Animal handed him a slip of paper.

The valet shook his head and whistled. "No wonder you can't get a ride. Nobody goes down that way if they ain't from there, especially tourists. What you want in Liberty City, brah?"

"What I want down there is my business and if you can't get me there then ain't no need in your worrying about it." Animal said.

"Ain't no need to get in your feelings. I didn't mean no disrespect, brah. Like I said, I might be able to help you. You need a ride and I got a car. I can run you to Liberty City for a few dollars." The valet explained.

"What, you the valet and a taxi driver?" Animal asked sarcastically.

The valet laughed. "Nah, man. I ain't no taxi. I'm just a lil short on gas money."

Animal pulled a brick of money from his pocket and peeled off two hundred-dollar bills. "Will this put enough gas in your car to get me to Liberty City?"

The valet's eyes got wide at the sight of the money. "Shit, for two hundred dollars I'll drive your ass all the way to Cuba!" the valet reached for the money, but Animal snatched it back.

"Just because I'm a tourist doesn't mean I'm stupid. You'll get your money when we reach Liberty City." Animal said.

"No problem, boss. Look, my shift is over in ten minutes. Meet me right here and I'll get you where you need to go."

Fifteen minutes later Animal and the valet were in a beat-up Honda Civic on I-195W heading deeper into the heart of Miami. The view of the city skyline as they crossed the Julia Tuttle Causeway was breathtaking. Most of his trip to Miami had been spent below decks or crossing through bad weather so he never really had a chance to appreciate the scenery.

"Your first time in the dirty?" the valet asked Animal.

"Huh?"

"I said is it your first time down south?"

"Nah, I been down bottom a few times, but never to Miami." Animal told him and went back to staring out the widow.

"You from up north, ain't you?" It was obvious that Animal wasn't interested in talking, but the valet was persistent.

"What makes you say that?" Animal asked.

"Your accent."

Animal gave him a quizzical look. "My accent? I think y'all the ones with accents."

"That's because you ain't from the south. To us you northerners are the ones who talk funny. You know what I'm saying, *kid*?" the valet did his best New York accent. He expected Animal to laugh, but he didn't. "So what part of the north are you from? D.C.? Philly? Nah, you a New York nigga."

"I'm from everywhere and nowhere. Why you asking me so many fucking questions, homie? You wired?" Animal said in an irritated tone.

"My fault, boss. I was just trying to make small talk." The valet said in an apologetic tone.

"Well, I ain't really the talking kid, feel me? So, if it's all the same to you, just get me to my destination." Animal turned his attention back to the window.

The valet must've gotten the hint because he was quiet for the rest of the ride. Animal enjoyed the sights and sounds of Miami. He had had a lot on his mind and it felt good just to be able to think for a minute. When he happened to look up and saw that they had crossed N.E. 59th street he started to pay more attention to his surroundings. The address he had given him was a park off N.E. 63rd and 2nd Avenue, so they would arrive at his destination in a few minutes. To his surprise the valet turned on N.E. 60th and started heading further west. Animal didn't know much about Miami, but he had googled the directions before he left the hotel, so he knew they were going in the wrong direction.

"My nigga, you could've gone up 2nd avenue and we'd have run into it." Animal pointed out.

"I know, boss, but at this time of day there would've been too much traffic. I'm taking a short cut. Relax yaself. I got this." The valet assured him.

The valet's words were calm and reassuring, too calm in fact. Animal's instincts were going crazy, but he kept his composure. Animal would be the first to admit that in light of everything that had happened he'd become highly paranoid and sometimes read too deep into things, but this didn't feel right. The valet made a sharp turn down a street that was lined with abandoned houses and killed the engine. Even before he saw men start to file out of one of the houses Animal knew what time it was. He had been caught slipping.

Animal turned to the valet who had produced a gun, seemingly out of thin air, and pointed it at him.

"What the fuck is this?" Animal asked, already knowing the answer to the question.

The valet tossed a copy of Animal's mix tape at him and smiled. "Like ya man Jay-Z said, *you got a face too easy to trace.* I pegged you from the moment I saw you at the hotel. There's big money on your head, superstar, and I aim to collect."

One of the men who had come out of the abandoned house snatched the passenger door open and jammed a 9mm into Animal's face. "You know what it is, nigga. Get the fuck out the car."

Animal looked to the valet. "If you know who I am then you know this ain't gonna end well for you. "

The valet nodded his head in agreement. "Yeah, you a big bad killer. Good thing that the reward is the same whether you're dead or alive. I'd rather take you back breathing, but I'm getting paid regardless."

Pain exploded in Animal's skull as the man holding the 9mm hit him in the side of the head. "Stop stalling and get the fuck out of the car before I blast you, brah!" The man ordered.

Animal clutched his head. Blood spilled over his fingers and down the side of his face from the gash that the gun had opened up. He glared murderously at the valet. "After I kill your boys, I'm gonna cut your lying tongue outta your fucking mouth."

"A gangsta, even in the face of impending doom. I respect you, brah, but I respect my pockets more. Take this nigga." The valet told his goons.

Animal knew that it was now or never, so when the man holding the 9mm reached for him, he made his move. He grabbed the arm holding the gun and pulled the man forward at the same time throwing his head backwards. Animal head butted the shocked gunman and busted his nose like an overripe tomato. Before the gunman could recover, Animal broke his arm at the elbow, causing the gun to go off. The stray bullet hit the valet in the nuts and he howled in pain as he flung himself out of the car. Hands reached into the car grabbing Animal by his hair and shirt, dragging him out of the vehicle.

They threw Animal to the floor and rat-packed on him. They kicked, stomped, and punch Animal all over his body. Somewhere in the mess of arms and legs Animal saw someone pull a knife, but there were so many of them beating on Animal that he couldn't get a clean-cut in. A few feet away he could see the valet crawling around on the ground, holding the bloody hole in his lap and crying hysterically. Animal managed to force a smile to his lips, right before someone kicked him in the mouth. There was no doubt in Animal's mind that he was living his final moments, but at least he would die with the vision of the valet's pain twisted face in his head.

When Animal heard the gunshot, his eyes automatically closed and his body went rigid. There were three more retorts from the gun and it he knew the game had officially come to an end for him. He waited for the searing pain that came with getting shot but didn't feel anything, which he attributed to his body being in shock from the beating. This drew his attention to the fact that he was no longer being beaten.

Animal opened one eye and found himself face to face with the corpse of the man who had hit him with the 9mm. Ignoring the pain in his body; he rolled away from the corpse and brushed against another one. From the tattoo on his hand he knew this had been the man holding the knife he'd seen. Animal propped himself up and took stock of his surroundings. All of his attackers were dead. Standing in the midst of the carnage were two people, a guy and a girl.

The girl was dark skinned with dyed blonde hair, accented with pink streaks, which she wore in two Princess Leia buns on either side of her head. She was petite in build but standing on the black and yellow roller skates she towered over her partner. She wore black leggings with a yellow sweatshirt that hung off one shoulder and was cut off at the stomach, showing off the tattoo just above her bellybutton that read *Uniquely Me In All Ways*. She reminded Animal of one of the girls from the old roller derby shows he used to watch with his aunt and uncle back in the days. She skated tight circles around her partner with her eyes locked on Animal the whole time.

The man was the complete opposite of the girl. Where as she was flashy, he was quiet and reserved. He wore a white shirt and black tie, under a simple black suit that hung perfectly on his wiry frame. His hair was cut low into a wavy Caesar with a half moon part carved into the left side of it. He looked like a little boy on his way home from church, except instead of a bible he carried a smoking 10mm.

The young man in the suit stepped through the bodies and hovered over Animal. He wasn't aiming the gun at him, but the tenseness in his hand said that he could bring it into play at a moment's notice. He studied Animal for a few minutes before extending his free hand.

Animal was hesitant.

The young man in the suit sighed and the girl rolled her eyes. He held the gun up to show Animal he meant him no harm then slipped it back into the holster beneath his jacket. He extended his hand again. This time Animal accepted the help to his feet.

"Are you hurt?" the young man in the suit asked.

"Just my pride." Animal brushed the dirt from his clothes. His body ached all over, but he was alive. "Thanks for saving my ass."

"No thanks needed, brother. I'm your unofficial guardian angel while you're in Miami." The young man in the suit informed him. He noticed the quizzical look on Animal's face. "Where are my manors? I'm called Brother Minister Jackson."

"Minister? What're you, some kind of Muslim?" Animal looked at his suit.

"Yes, I'm a Muslim, but Minister is actually my first name. Don't ask because I'm not going to explain." Minister told him. "This," he pointed to the girl on the roller skates, "is Unique." Unique gave Animal a shy smile. "We're associates of Diamonds."

Animal frowned. "So, what was this shit? Some kind of test?"

"I assure you, brother, this was none of our doing. Diamonds doesn't do tests. Either you're with him or you're not." Minister said seriously. "We've been tailing you since you got off the boat to see if you were who you said you were and to make sure you got to where you needed to be."

"So, am I who I'm supposed to be?" Animal asked sarcastically.

"Judging by the fact that you're standing in the middle of a crime scene within a few hours of landing in Miami, I'd say you're the man they call Animal. I want to apologize to you for slipping in my responsibilities. Had we not lost track of you in traffic these cats would've never gotten within three feet of you." Minister said.

"I'd rather you showed up late than not at all. Any idea who these guys are?"

Minister shrugged. "Just some knuckleheads who tried to come up off a tourist."

Unique slammed one of the heavy roller skates into the valet's side. "Too bad this tourist was under the protection of Diamonds." Unique squatted over the injured valet. She produced a blade from her bra and placed it to the valet's throat.

"Please, I didn't know he was with Diamonds." The valet tried to explain.

"Too bad, too sad." Unique cut him across the cheek. She took the bloody knife and smeared the letter U on the valet's forehead. "This is gonna be fun."

"Unique, stop playing. Kill him and be done with it. Diamonds is waiting on us and you know he's impatient." Minister told her.

"Alright, alright, freaking spoil sport." Unique mumbled. She tightened the grip on the knife, prepared to finish the valet off.

"Wait!" Animal called out.

Unique scowled at Animal. "What the fuck do you mean wait? This guy tried to off you and you wanna spare him?"

Animal approached them. "Absolutely not. This lying piece of shit is going to die, but I just wanted to do the honors. That is, if you don't mind?"

"Not at all," Unique smiled and placed the bloody knife in Animal's hand.

The valet took one look at the murderous look in Animal's eyes and pissed his pants. "Please, I'm sorry. I swear if you let me live you'll never see me again."

"Stop fucking crying!" Unique kicked the valet in his head roughly with the skate.

The valet's eyes rolled back in his head like he was going to pass out, but Animal slapped him twice hard across the face. "Nah, I need you to be wide awake for this." Animal squeezed the valet's cheeks, forcing his mouth open. He placed the blade on the valet's tongue. "Unlike you, I'm a man of my word." He told him before cutting his tongue out.

"Are you quite done?" Minister didn't bother to hide his disgust at Animal's brutality.

"I recon so." Animal wiped the blade on the valet's uniform and handed it back to Unique. "Thank you."

"Let's get out of here. Diamonds is waiting for us." Minister led the trio back up the block to where their car was parked.

As they walked up the street, Unique skated up next to Animal. "I think I'm gonna like you." She winked and skated away.

CHAPTER 2

Ashanti sat in the window of the fifth - floor apartment, staring out the rain streaked window. It was coming down pretty hard, but he was dressed for the weather. Green army jacket, black boots and a safari cap. His hand was shoved deep into the pocket of his army jacket, where he absently stroked the small .38 he was carrying. He was ready for anything man or nature had to throw at him.

Ashanti's keen eyes were locked on the playground below, where a dude named Terror sat on the bench. A large umbrella sat on his shoulder, protecting him from the rain while he conducted his business. Terror was serving fiends like he had a license to do it. He was the only one bold or dumb enough to hustle out in the open after what had happened. The hood was a ghost town and it was all his fault.

The block was on fire with police doubling up their patrols and under covers lurking in every nook and cranny of the General Grant Houses. Their hourly sweeps made the hood hot and it only promised to get hotter before it was all said and done. The police were assholes as a rule, but this time even Ashanti had to admit they were justified in their anger. The act that had drawn down their wrath had been so heinous that it not only touched the hood, but rocked the whole city.

A few nights prior there had been a dice game on the Avenue that had attracted a small crowd of hustlers from the hood, including Terror. Terror wasn't originally from the projects, but he had been living there for years. He and his younger brother had come to New York to live with their grandmother after their parents were tragically killed in a bank robbery gone wrong. Both brothers were criminals, but Terror's antics put him in a class by himself. He was a reckless young bull who had no value for his life or anyone else's, which ostracized him from most clicks, but Terror didn't need a click. He was a one-man army. Most of the crews steered clear of the violent youth, including King James. Terror was a federal case in the making and King wanted no parts of it.

Terror had been on a rotten streak and was getting tight that the young boy who was holding the bank was taking all his money. They started off slinging playful insults at each other, but it wasn't long before the insults turned into sharp words. It didn't take long before lines and weapons were drawn with Terror on one side and the kid and his crew on the other. The kid holding the bank had numbers on his side so he expected Terror to back down. That's because he didn't know Terror.

Without so much as a second though, Terror opened fire. The kid he'd been arguing with was knocked out of his shoes and his friends ran for cover. Terror fired recklessly at the fleeing men, but missed his targets. He did manage to hit a little girl who had just come out of the store. She was buying milk and cereal for her little brothers and sisters when a stray bullet cut her down just shy of her thirteenth birthday.

The story of her murder was broadcast on every major news station. There was an outcry for justice for the senseless slaying of the little black girl that could be heard in ghettos across America. The police suspected that it had been Terror who had been responsible for the shooting, but they had no way to prove it. Everyone was too frightened of Terror to speak out against him, so the police couldn't touch him.

Most people in the neighborhood took the girl's murder hard, but Ashanti took it personal. She was cool little chick who he would often send to the store for him to put a few dollars in her pockets. He loved to hear her tell stories of how she was going to become a doctor one day and get her family out of the hood. Terror had killed her dreams and it sickened Ashanti to see him strutting around like he was untouchable while in the next building a mother mourned the loss of her child.

"If looks could kill, I think ol' boy would've fallen over dead by now." King James startled Ashanti as he hadn't heard him approach. He was dressed in a black hoodie and black Yankee fitted cap. His signature rope chain with the crescent moon medallion hung around his neck.

"Huh?" Ashanti turned to King James.

King James nodded out the window at Terror. "I see you shooting prisons at that cat. I don't blame you. Scrams is a slimy nigga."

"The slimiest." Ashanti said. "They were trying to send my nigga Animal to the gas chamber for killing a few pieces of shit, but Terror murks a kid and gets to walk around free. It ain't right, King."

"Yeah, shit is foul, but what can you do? Terror needs to be punished but the police can't touch him unless somebody steps forward." King James said.

"Somebody needs to do something."

"So, what? You gonna snitch on the nigga so justice can be served?" King James asked.

"Fuck no. Snitching ain't nowhere in my character. You know that, King." Ashanti told him. "I just think something needs to be done, man."

"I agree. Terror has brought a lot of heat on this hood with his bullshit. It was already hard to get a dollar, but these knockers and these sweeps are gonna drive us all to the poor house. Shit, I ain't gotta tell you that because the soldiers are getting the worse of it. If we can't clock, we can't pay y'all. I was even talking to Lakim this morning about how we might have to let a few niggaz go off the payroll until all this gets worked out." King James told him.

"That's fuck up. I know a lot of dudes who are gonna go hungry if they can't get a dollar with the team." Ashanti said.

"Yeah, it's a hard pill to swallow, but what can we do? The only way to get the heat off of us is to get rid of Terror, but if the police can't touch him what other choice do we have?" King paused as if he was deep in thought. "You know, there's quite a few cats who would find themselves mighty grateful if somebody were to knock Terror out the box."

"What? You talking about killing him?" Ashanti asked.

King James raised his hands in surrender. "Hey, you didn't hear me say nothing about killing anybody. All I said is that folks would be grateful if he wasn't here anymore, feel me?" he gave Ashanti a look.

Ashanti nodded. "Yeah, I feel you."

King James patted Ashanti on the back. "Good. I'm gonna dip to the Bronx for a few hours to handle some business. Give me a shout if anything *interesting* goes down on the block while I'm not around." King James left Ashanti alone with his thoughts.

Ashanti continued sitting in the window, staring down at Terror. King James' words played in his head and he knew what time it was without the big homie having to say so. He was being tested. Ashanti had never been any good at test in school, but this one he would pass with flying colors.

Ashanti pulled himself away from the window and started across the living room. The homies were all sitting around passing blunts and talking shit. Standing in the doorway of the kitchen holding a coffee pot full of murky water was a girl named Fatima who worked for King James. She was about the same age as Ashanti, but stacked like a woman in her twenties. Ashanti's hart always beat a little faster whenever he saw her. Ashanti had been infatuated with Fatima from the first time he laid eyes on her, but never got up the courage to tell her. Fatima must've felt him staring because she looked up at him and smiled. Ashanti returned the smile before putting his head down nervously and continuing towards the door.

The homies flooded the living room, bagging up, counting money or bullshitting. At their usual positions, in front of the television playing video games were Meek and Dee. They were two young boys on the fast track. Meek was a good dude, but he didn't have the killer edge that it took to become a ghetto star. Dee, on the other hand showed promise. He was about his money when he wasn't killing his brain cells with weed and video games.

Sitting on the couch with his face buried in a Newspaper and a green highlighter tucked behind his ear, was Alonzo aka Zo-Pound. Zo was like a big brother to Ashanti and the closest thing to a friend he had left. When Zo noticed Ashanti storming out of the apartment he looked up from his reading.

"Where you headed, my nigga?" Alonzo asked.

"Gotta see a man about a morality test." Ashanti told him and left the apartment.

All Alonzo could do was shake his head at Ashanti's statement. If he knew him as well as he thought he did, *morality test* was probably code for mischief. Causing mischief was what Ashanti did best. His wild ways and abrasive attitude soured a lot of people on Ashanti, but the hood niggaz loved him, especially Alonzo. He was like the little brother he never had.

Alonzo was about to go back to his newspaper when it was abruptly snatched from his hands. He looked up, ready to flip, but his anger died when he saw that it was Fatima. She was one of King James' top chefs, highly skilled in the art of turning cocaine into crack. At seventeen years old she could cook drugs better than cats that had been doing it for years.

Fatima was a young brown skinned chick with a pretty smile and ass for days. The young beauty was highly coveted in the hood, but only the bold or stupid tried to get with her. Fatima was a master at manipulating men to further her own gains. When she was done she would toss them to the side like toys she had gotten bored with. Being played by a child didn't go over well with her victims, but none of them dared try to get out of pocket. Not only was she the daughter of a notorious killer, but she was like a play sister to King James. Since he'd come home from prison he and Fatima had been spending a lot of time together. Some speculated that their relationship was more intimate than they let on, but nobody would say it out loud.

"Fatima, why do you play so much? Give it back." Alonzo reached for the newspaper but she snatched it out of his reach.

"I'm just trying to see what you're reading that's so interesting." Fatima looked at the newspaper and frowned at the sections Alonzo had highlighted. "The classified ads?"

"Yes." Alonzo snatched the newspaper back from her and smoothed it out on the table.

Fatima sat on the table so that she was facing him. "Zo, you're a strange dude."

"Why is that?" he asked.

"Because with all this money we making in the trap I can't understand why you'd be looking for a job." Fatima said.

"Because the trap don't last forever, ma. You gotta have something to fall back on." Alonzo told her.

"That's why you stack your bread, so when you retire you're caked up." Fatima said as if it was that simple.

Alonzo pushed the newspaper to the side and gave Fatima his undivided attention. "How many retired drug dealers do you know?"

Fatima thought on it for a few seconds. "None."

"Exactly, you don't retire from this shit, it retires *you*. I ain't one of those dudes who is gonna be out here hustling until somebody puts a bullet in his head or his ass in a cage. I'm trying to land a gig so I can start putting my life together and live like a square."

Fatima laughed. "Zo, I've got more of a chance at being a man than you have at living like a square." She placed her hand over his heart. "It ain't in you. We're young superstars and *that* world ain't big enough for people like us."

"Then it had better make room." Alonzo got up from the couch, tucking his newspaper under his arm. He made tracks from the apartment without saying anything to anyone because he wasn't sure if he'd be able to hide the fact that Fatima had hit a nerve. Alonzo knew that getting off the streets and getting a job was the right thing to do, but the right thing wasn't putting food in his stomach. He'd promised himself that hustling with his brother and King James would only be a temporary arrangement but the deeper he got the more of the old him crept back to the surface. He could hear the streets moaning in his ears and was getting seduced by her. He wondered when the moment came when he had to choose between the life of a square versus that of an outlaw, would he be able to make the right decision?

Alonzo decided to take a walk to the store to clear his head. As he stood at the end of the hallway pressing for the elevator he could hear raised voices coming from a few floors below. He was about to ignore it and continue with his business until he heard the familiar pop of a gunshot. His brain immediately shifted to war mode and before he knew it he was hitting the staircase to investigate.

Terror sat on the bench in front of building 550, watching the block watch him. When Terror was around the hood was always tense because you never knew what he was going to do and who he was going to do it to. It kept everyone edgy around him and he preferred it like that.

Playing the hood openly like that with all the heat on him wasn't the smartest thing to do but Terror had never been known for his brains. The increased police presence in the hood forced everyone else to either close shop completely or scale back which left the lane open for Terror. The fiends flocked to him like blind mice because he was the only one holding the cheese.

Terror was just serving a fiend the last of his package when he saw King James come out of the lobby with his pet pit bull, Lakim, trailing a few paces behind him. Of all the dudes who claimed to be getting money uptown, King James was one of the few Terror respected. Terror was the new kid on the block when King James had gone away, but even back then King was a young beast. King was a gladiator, same as Terror, and he felt a kinship with his warrior spirit. He'd reached out to King James a few times about doing business, but King always spun him with a promise to follow up that he never kept.

"Fuck that nigga too." Terror said to no one in particular, diddy-bopping towards the building to go re-up.

Instead of taking the elevator, Terror hit the stairs like he always did. He hated elevators because they were too easy to get trapped off in. He had caught more than his fair share of people in them so he knew this first hand. At the same time he was going up the stairs someone was coming down. He immediately recognized little Ashanti. They weren't friends to speak of, but Terror knew him from when he used to run around with Brasco robbing cats uptown. The last he'd heard, Ashanti had taken up with King James and his crew so that unofficially put him on Terror's shit list. He didn't like the way Ashanti was looking at him so he decided to fuck with him.

"Sup, lil nigga?" Terror asked in a threatening voice. Ashanti didn't say a word. He just continued staring at Terror. "Fuck is your problem?"

Ashanti pulled his little .38 and pointed it at Terror. Ashanti's mouth was so dry that he couldn't answer if he wanted to. He was no stranger to putting in work, but that was in the heat of battle. This was cold blooded murder.

Terror gave a throaty laugh. "I get it. Ya boss wants me out the box but he was too much of a pussy to step to me himself, so he sends the help? Shorty, I'm gonna take that hammer and fuck you in the ass with it before I shove it in King James' mouth." Terror reached for the gun and his shoulder exploded with pain. He staggered back with a startled expression on his face as if he had been slapped unexpectedly. He touched his hand to his shoulder and when his fingertips came away slick with blood, his shock turned to anger. "I was just gonna kick your ass, but now I'm gonna kill you."

Terror lunged for Ashanti. Ashanti tried to get off another shot, but Terror moved faster than he had expected. The larger man wrapped Ashanti in a tight bear hug and applied pressure. Ashanti heard his back crack loudly right before his hands went numb. It felt like Terror was trying to snap his spine and there was no doubt that he would succeed unless Ashanti did something. He head-butted Terror so hard that he almost knocked himself out, but Terror held fast. Ashanti could feel himself getting dizzy from lack of oxygen but all he could do was hang there like a rag doll while Terror crushed him. Just when he felt the lights going out, Terror suddenly released him.

Ashanti lay on the steps gasping for air, while thanking God that he wasn't dead. When he looked up at Terror, his face was twisted into a mask of pain. He was reaching over his shoulder for something that he couldn't quite get hold of, cursing. There was a wet sound like meat being cleaved and Terror dropped to his knees. Standing just behind him, holding a bloody knife was Ashanti's savior, Alonzo.

"Ashanti what the fuck is going on?" Alonzo asked with a shocked expression on his face. The last thing he expected to see when he came down the stairs was Ashanti getting his ass handed to him.

The split second it took Alonzo to question Ashanti was all that Terror needed to regroup. "I'm gonna kill all you fucking roaches." Terror roared as he sprung to his feet. Alonzo was caught totally off guard when Terror grabbed him around his legs and lifted him into the air. Alonzo hit him twice more in the side with the knife, but Terror was un-phased. The next thing he knew they were both airborne and flying down the stairs. When they hit the wall on the landing below Alonzo took the worse of the impact and the knife flew out of his hand and put him at Terror's mercy.

Alonzo delivered a quick combination to Terror's face that would've have laid most men out, but Terror ate the punches like they were snacks. Terror pinned Alonzo to the wall by his throat and punched him in his exposed face. Alonzo had been in plenty of fistfights against opponents who were bigger than him, but they all failed in comparison to Terror. Even with a bullet in

his shoulder he was still as strong as an ox. Every time
he hit Alonzo it felt like he had been bitch slapped by
the Incredible Hulk. Alonzo raised his hands to protect
his face leaving his midsection open and Terror went to
work. Every blow that landed shifted his intestines.

Ashanti finally managed to compose himself
enough to rejoin the fight. He scooped up the .38 and
let off two shots, both of which hit Terror high in his
broad back. The .38 might as well have been a pellet
gun because it seemed to only annoy Terror. He
abandoned his pummeling of Alonzo and turned his
attention back to Ashanti. Ashanti pointed the gun at
Terror's face and pulled the trigger, but nothing
happened. The gun was empty. At first, he couldn't
understand it, but then he remembered that he had been
clowning around on the roof with Meek and Dee,
letting shots off in the air earlier that day and he'd
forgotten to make sure the gun was fully loaded when

he went after Terror. It was a rookie mistake that was about to cost him.

Not sure what else to do Ashanti rushed Terror and slammed the empty .38 against the side of his head over and over until he drew blood. Terror woozy, so when he swung on Ashanti, it was awkward and easy to dodge. Balancing himself between the wall and the banister, Ashanti bunched his knees to his chest and shot his legs out, kicking Terror in the chest. Terror stumbled down the stairs right into Alonzo, who had retrieved his knife.

Terror swung high, but Alonzo went low. He hit Terror in the gut once with the knife then struck him twice more on his inner thigh, aiming for his femoral artery. Terror swung his massive fists like a club trying to take Alonzo's head off, but Alonzo was quicker. He pushed the blade through Terror's forearm before brining it around and stabbing him in the soft flesh between his collarbone and neck. Terror went down to one knee, bleeding like a stuck pig but was still trying to fight his way to his feet. If nothing else, Terror had the will of a titan.

Alonzo's legs felt like noodles when he moved to step behind Terror, placing the blade against his neck. He had to respect the man because if nothing else he had the heart of a titan, but respect or not Terror had to go. "Fucking die already," he slit Terror's throat.

Terror's body twitched and flapped around for almost a full three minutes before he was finally still. Ashanti sat on the steps, elbows on his knees gasping for air. He looked over at Alonzo, who sat on the floor in the corner of the landing, with his head propped against a wall. Alonzo was still, but his eyes burned holes in Ashanti.

"If I could stand up, I'd kick your ass for getting me caught up in this." Alonzo told him. He was winded and his body ached so bad that he felt like it would be at least a week before he could move.

"And if I had any bullets left in my gun, I'd shoot you the minute you tried." Ashanti replied.

After a few more minutes the two battle worn comrades staggered to their feet and made slow, painful, steps from the scene of the crime. Alonzo's ribs hurt so bad that he had to stop twice before they had even made it off the block. He was pretty sure that he needed medical attention, but there was no way he was going to the hospital after what they had done. A simple walk to the store had turned into a homicide. "What the fuck am I doing with my life?"

"Who you talking to, Zo?" Ashanti asked.

Alonzo looked down at his bloody clothes. "I don't even know anymore."

CHAPTER 3

During the ride to their destination, Unique was quiet, but Animal could feel her watching him from the backseat. Minister gave Animal the play by play on the city of Miami, occasionally throwing in a splash of his life. He was originally from Philadelphia, but had relocated to Miami when he'd gotten out of the service. He and his brother had been partners in a private security firm that was funded by his brother's drug money. Minister wanted to go all the way legit, but his brother was too turned out by the life to give it up. He wanted to be a rock star, while Minister just wanted to make money. Minister brought in some of his old military comrades and formed an efficient security team and the demand soon grew as did the company. Being that Minister seemed to have a handle on the company, it left his brother time to run the streets. It wasn't long before his brother's name had started ringing and Minister had received the phone call he had been dreading. His brother was killed. As the story went he had been gunned down during a dispute over one hundred dollars and a gril.

His brother's death had been a wake-up call for Minister and he threw himself completely into the company. Minister and his team accepted clients from all walks of life, so long as they had the money to pay for their services, but they catered to celebrities. Miami had become the new *it* spot, always flush with big spenders who wanted to sample it's forbidden fruits, but its allure is also was also one of the reasons why it was so dangerous. No matter how much money you had, you couldn't really enjoy it unless you were plugged in. This is where Minister and his crew came in. They provided the connections and protection required to make you stay in the sunshine state a comfortable one.

By the time they arrived at the destination and Minister had finished his rundown, Animal had a whole new respect for the young man in the suit.

Minister drove them to a rundown strip off N.W. 79th street, where he pulled the car into a narrow parking lot between a small carpet store and a rickety looking blocked shaped building that appeared to be undergoing some kind of renovation. Scaffolding snaked around the lower level of the building to catch the debris from the work they were doing on the roof. Most of the original paint had been sandblasted off and was being replaced by a fresh coat of purple paint. Why someone would paint a building purple was beyond Animal. The place had seen better days, but someone was making an effort to restore it. Hanging on the side of the building was a burnt-out sign that had once read *Foxxy Lady Lounge*, but like everything else since Diamonds had hit the scene, it would soon be replaced.

"This it?" Animal asked looking up at the structure.

"This is it." Minister confirmed and got out of the car. Unique and Animal followed.

Minister led them around to the front of the building, side stepping buckets of paint and loose wires. The place appeared to be under construction, but still open for business. The loose pockets of stragglers hanging out in front parted for Minister.

Animal was hesitant about following him inside. The place felt menacing, and all his scruples told him to be somewhere else, but his heart pushed him forward.

"You're good here, " Unique picked up on his apprehension.

The inside of the place was more polished than the outside. The foyer was clean and lined with a brand-new carpet which was the same deeps shade of purple as the outside. Minister stood just outside the cloak room speaking with two men. They were both sinister looking, one appearing older than the other. The elder was of salt and pepper hair with a white patch covering his right eye. The younger a bit on the scruffier side, sporting his hair wild and uncombed with a free growing beard. The hair covering his jaw was thinner on the left as a result of once getting peppered with buckshot's to the face. When he opened his mouth to respond to whatever Minster was saying, Animal spied a mouth full of pointed gold teeth. They made him look like a predator.

"Don't stare. He hates it when people stare." Unique whispered. "Minister will take you to meet Diamonds and I'll see you guys in the back. Don't disappear on me, cutie." Unique winked and skated away.

"Animal." Minister approached, with the other man trailing him. "This is Blue, one of our comrades." He introduced Animal to the man wearing the white patch.

Blue gave Animal the once over with his good eye and smirked. "Funny, from all that I've heard about you'd I expected you to be a lot bigger."

"You know what they say; it ain't the size of the dog, but the fight in him." Animal replied cooly.

Blue laughed and gave Animal a firm slap on the back. "I like this lil nigga. Y'all come on in the back so we can get with Diamonds." Blue walked off and stepped through the curtain that led to the interior of the club.

Animal made to follow, but Minister stopped him. "What brought you to this place isn't my business, but I dig you so I'm gonna give you some friendly advice.

Be sure this is what you want before you play
Diamonds' game.

"Minister, I appreciate your honesty, so let me be
completely honest with you. I've come too far to turn
back even if I wanted to." Animal stepped passed him
and parted the curtains.

When Animal appeared on the other side of the veil
he was taken aback. He found himself standing in the
middle of a large room that spanned the length of the
building. Animal had to give his eyes a minute to
adjust because he had never in his life seen so much
purple. The floors, the walls, even the fluorescent
lights that ringed the bar were tinted purple with a flash
of hot pinks and blues thrown in. It felt like an acid trip
gone wrong, but Animal couldn't deny the fact that the
place was different.

Standing on the bar was a thick pecan colored
stallion, wearing little more than a few strips of cloth

that were supposed to pass for a bikini. The place wasn't that crowded because it was early but the few dudes who were there crowded around the bar watching the girl do her thing. She had all their attentions held fast, but her focus was on the stranger who had just entered the room. The light bounced off strange purple contacts she was wearing making her eyes seem to glow. Animal wanted to turn away, but there was something about the dancer that wouldn't allow him to. He had taken two steps towards the bar when Minister laid a hand on his shoulder.

"Stay focused, brother. Your business is with Diamonds, not Reign." Minister steered Animal back the other way.

"What is this place?" Animal asked, trying not to look over his shoulder at Reign.

"Purple City. When it's finished it'll be a circus within a circus of a city. But why I don't let the ring master tell you about it himself?" Minister led Animal deeper into the club.

Half a dozen men lounged at a table in the back. Animal recognized the joker with the gold fangs, but the man he was trading secrets with was unfamiliar. Long dreadlocks obscured his face, but Animal could feel his dark eyes on him. That had to be Diamonds.

CHAPTER 4

Alonzo had planned to just kick it in the crib for the rest of the night until he'd gotten the call from Lakim. King James wanted them to meet up in the hood about a situation. Alonzo played dumb but he knew what it was about. Someone had found the body he and Ashanti left in the lobby of the stash spot. Lakim didn't sound happy, but neither was Zo so he was cool with it going either way.

When he reached the block he found a full house; King James, Lakim, Dee, Meek and Ashanti were all huddled under the elevated train tracks. They were focused one something across the street that he couldn't see yet.

As Alonzo got closer he could hear shouting. Everyone's attention seemed to be focused on a neighborhood kid who was seemed to be high of something he couldn't control. A liquor bottle hung from one hand and a gun from the other., while the drunk raged. He was agitated and ready to make a bad decision.

"What the fuck is going on?" Alonzo asked.

"The young boy is tripping. He been at it for about a half hour." King James informed him.

"Who the hell is he?" Alonzo was curious to know

"Zodiah." Meek said as if he was about to recount a ghost story. "He calls him self General Zod and the boy is a certified juvenile delinquent. He plays with them *thangs* heavy, which is why I'm surprised you don't know him, Zo. Guns were your game, weren't they?"

"A long time ago." Alonzo said. "Nah, I don't know the kid. What's he tripping off?"

"Family." Dee picked up the story. "Somebody killed his big brother earlier and when Zod found out he lost it. I heard he got a hold of one of those dipped cigarettes and came out here on some Wild Bill shit. He said he gonna keep it turned up on the hood until somebody comes forward about who killed his brother. I believe him too. He shot one nigga already since we were standing out here. Him and his brother were close."

"Who was his brother?" Alonzo asked, fearing he already knew the answer.

"A kid named Terror. You knew him?" King James studied Alonzo's face.

"Nah, I didn't know him. I'd only started hearing about him after he shot the lil girl." The lie rolled so fluidly off Alonzo's tongue that he almost believed it.

King James continued. "They found him shot and stabbed in the stairwell of the building."

Ashanti whistled. "Damn, shot and stabbed?
Somebody must've wanted him outta the way pretty
bad."

"Seems so." King James said.

"This nigga is making the block hotter than it
already is with all this shooting. What you wanna do
about this nigga, King?" Lakim asked.

King James nodded at the blue and white police car
that had just pulled up. "We ain't gotta do shit but sit
back and watch the festivities. This should be
interesting."

Zod had been knee deep in the guts of a pretty
Spanish girl when he'd gotten the dreaded call. He
ignored the phone the first few times it rung, but on the

third time picked it up. When his little homie had told him of his discovery his whole body went numb. His big brother Terror had been a God in his eyes and somebody had killed him.

The first thing he did was hit the block to confirm the rumor. Sure enough, when he arrived he found the building taped off and his grandmother on the sidelines being consoled by neighbors, while the police questioned her. He was so broken up that he couldn't face her. He had no words that would ease her pain. The only thing he could think of that would make this right was murder.

He went to see his man on the Eastside and bought three cigarettes dipped in PCP. Zod generally didn't do anything harder than weed or alcohol but he needed something extra that night. He had never done PCP and was caught unprepared for the freight train that slammed into his brain halfway through the first cigarette. It was as if he was standing outside his body, watching himself slip on a bullet proof vest and grab his brother's favorite .44 Taurus off the dresser.

Zod's body was on fire and he desperately needed air. He stepped outside with a frown on his face and rage in his heart, born of drugs and fueled by liquor. The PCP had his mind racing so fast that he couldn't slow his thoughts long enough to make sense of them. He stumbled out into the courtyard in front of the building. There were a few people out trying to enjoy the weather, despite the dark cloud of what happened earlier still lingering. Off to the side there was a young dude making a sale to the crack head. Zod didn't know him, but something about his face made him angry. He approached the kid with the .44 tucked behind his back.

"Yo." Zod called out. The kid looked around confused because he wasn't sure who Zod was talking to. "You mutha fucka!"

"You know me, scrap?" the kid asked with an attitude.

"Nah, I don't know you." Zod pulled the .44 and pointed it at the kid's face. "But I'm gonna get to know your thoughts if you don't tell me what happened with my brother."

"Man, I don't know you or your brother." The kid said nervously.

"Don't lie to me!" Zod raged. "Y'all niggaz in this hood never liked my brother and that's why y'all killed him! Y'all some jealous ass niggaz!"

"On everything I love I don't know nothing about nobody getting shot!" The kid tried to explain.

"Too bad, because if you can't tell me what I want to know then that makes you useless." Zod pulled the trigger. The bullet hit the kid in the shoulder and knocked him over the fence, which is probably the only thing that saved his life. Zod lost sight of him in the bushes and by the time he spotted him the kid was scrambling across the street, clutching his wounded shoulder. Zod fired after him but the kid was only gone.

The sound of gunshots made the few people who were in front of the park scatter like roaches. Seeing their panic excited Zod to the point where he had gotten an erection. Their fear was more potent than any drug he'd ever tried and he wanted more of it, so he fired at the fleeing people. "That's right, run like the scared lil bitches y'all are. This whole hood will kneel before General Zod for what y'all did to my brother!" he fired off another shot at the crowd. Thankfully he didn't hit anyone, but his point was made.

A blue and white police car jumped the curb and two officers spilled out with their guns drawn. They advanced on Zod but he didn't seem to care as he walked to meet them half way. "Oh, y'all want some of General Zod?" he his gun dangled at his side.

"Put the fucking gun down, now!" One of the officers ordered.

"Fuck you! I give the orders around here." Zod fired two shots and backed the police up to their car for cover. Two more police cars joined the first and they the officers returned fire at the crazed man with the .44. Zod just laughed, taking his time to reload the gun as the bullets whizzed by him. Once his gun was reloaded he got back to shooting at the police. He was so far in the throws of the PCP that it never even occurred to him that he was fighting a battle that he couldn't win.

The police returned fire, mostly missing, but one bullet grazed Zod's arm and temporarily brought him back to sanity and he realized the seriousness of his situation. Zod had opened fire on the police so even if he wanted to surrender wasn't an option. They meant to kill him, and he was more than ready to die, but not before his brother's death was avenged.

The police closed in on him from both ramps and over the fence that separated the playground from the street. Things were getting bad for Zod in a hurry. He backpedaled towards the building, occasionally letting off a shot at the police to keep them back. He knew he didn't have the firepower to go to war so his best bet was to make a grand escape. He yanked at the handle of the lobby door and surprisingly it was locked. The lobby door lock had been broken all summer and it was just his luck that they fixed it when he needed it to be broken most. Luckily a woman was coming out at the same time he was trying to get in. Zod grabbed her in a reverse chokehold and used her as a shield to keep the police at bay.

"You come any closer and I'm gonna waste this bitch!" Zod told the advancing officers. He made sure to keep her in front of him incase one of the cops got trigger happy.

"Please, I got three babies to get home to. Don't do this." The woman pleaded.

"Lady, trust me I've got no intentions on harming you. If I had any other choice it wouldn't even be going down like this, but if I let you go they're gonna kill me. Just stay cool and we can both make it out of this alive." Zod told her.

"Let the lady go." One of the cops closest to him shouted to Zod. He inched ever closer to the gunman.

Zod fired a shot in his direction to back him up. "I'll let your brains go if you don't back the fuck up!"

Still holding the woman in front of him, Zod reached behind him and pulled the lobby door open. He backed up into the lobby, sweeping his gun back and forth at the police advancing on both sides. When he was clear, he pushed the woman outside, slammed the lobby door and headed for the rear exit. Zod felt bad about the woman, but the ends justified the means and she served her purpose. If he could make it out the back of the building he was home free.

Zod jumped down the short flight of steps leading to the back door and kicked it open. When he felt the cool air on his face, he smiled knowing that he was in the clear. As soon as Zod stepped out of the rear exit and let the door close behind him, the smile faded as he found himself trapped by a dozen police officers, all aiming guns at him.

"Aw fuck!" was all Zod could say before they opened fire.

King James and his crew stood around with the rest of the spectators after the epic gun battle that had just taken place in their hood. Two paramedics, escorted by half dozen cops, wheeled Zod on a gurney to the waiting ambulance. Even after getting shot up and handcuffed, Zod was still carrying on like a lunatic.

"You mutha fuckas think you can hold me? Never. I'm General Zod. I'm invincible!" Zod babbled as he struggled against the cuffs that bound him to the gurney.

"Shut the fuck up." One of the officers escorting Zod jabbed him in the ribs with his nightstick, causing Zod to howl out in pain.

"Fuck you!" Zod foamed at the mouth and tried as hard as he could to get to the officer. "I'm General Zod; your court system has no power over me. I make the rules!" Zod ranted as they loaded him into the back of the ambulance. He was still going off the PCP and it would be a while before the seriousness of his situation set in. When he finally did become competent enough to stand before a judge Zod would realize that avenging his brother's murder would be the least of the problems he was facing.

"That nigga made a straight movie out here." Dee said as the y all watched the ambulance carrying Zod disappear into the night.

"He sure did. An urban tragedy." Lakim said.

"They gonna throw the book at him." Ashanti added.

"Maybe, maybe not. That boy was dusted up outta his mind. If he gets the right lawyer on the case, there may be some hope for his stupid ass." King James said.

"Well, now that his crazy ass is locked up there shouldn't be anymore backlash behind this, right?" Alonzo asked.

"Hard to say. Zod is out the box, but there's a lot of young dumb niggaz who follow his word like the gospel. My advice is for everybody to stay on point just incase anybody gets any big ideas." King James told his crew.

"But King, we ain't have nothing to do with Terror getting killed. It wouldn't make any sense for Zod or his people to bring the bullshit this way, would it?" Ashanti asked. He wasn't afraid, just curious as to how deep all this went.

King gave him a look. "You see for yourself what kinda cat that lil dude is. Does he strike you as person who does shit that makes sense?"

Ashanti thought on it. "I see your point."

"I figured you might. When all this shit dies down I want everybody back at their posts. Shop is officially back open." King James declared.

"What about the police? Ain't shit gonna be out around here?" Meek asked.

King James smirked at him. "We sell drugs, nigga. When is it not hot for us?"

Ashanti's phone vibrated in his pocket so he stepped away from the group to take the call. He looked at the caller I.D. and frowned because he didn't recognize the number. "Who this?" he answered with an attitude.

"Now is that anyway to greet the don of all dons?" a familiar voice said on the other end.

"Who is this, Don B.?" Ashanti asked in surprise.

"But of course." Don B. said.

"Blood, how did you even get my number?" It was a new phone and only those closest to Ashanti had the number.

"The don knows all and sees all. But skip all that. I need you to come meet me. I gotta holla at you about some business." Don B. told him.

Ashanti looked at the phone and rolled his eyes in disgust. "What kind of business we got, Don? You know I don't fuck wit y'all niggaz like that."

"You might not fuck with Big Dawg, but I know you fuck with Grants, Franklins and Jacksons, right?"

"I'm listening." Ashanti said.

"Not over the phone. Meet me by the Root spot on Seventh in half hour." Don B. said and hung up the phone before Ashanti could answer.

"Asshole." Ashanti said to the phone and slipped it back into his pocket.

"Who was that?" Alonzo crept up on Ashanti.

"Wrong number." Ashanti lied.

Alonzo clearly didn't believe him, but he didn't press it. "I'm about to go get some food from the Chinese joint then go upstairs and help these niggaz bag this work up. You coming?"

"Nah, I got a move to bust right quick, but I'll meet y'all at the apartment later." Ashanti gave Alonzo dap and made his exit.

Alonzo stood on the corner for a time watching Ashanti disappear off to God knows where. He knew he was going to meet whoever was on the other end of the phone, whoever that might've been. For as close as Ashanti and Zo-Pound might have been there was still a great deal that the youngster kept guarded. Alonzo wouldn't question him about it; he'd just make sure he was there with a listening ear when his friend was ready to talk about it.

CHAPTER 5

By the time Ashanti got to the Root spot, Don B's red Bentley Coupe was already idling at the curb. Devil leaned against the trunk of the car, arms folded, and chatting on a cell phone. Standing with his back to Ashanti, whispering to someone in the passenger seat, was Tone. Tone was Don B's assistant and childhood friend. The ear he whispered into belonged to the man who had *summoned* Ashanti, Don B.

The gangster turned music mogul, had the seat pushed back as far as it would go and had one white Nike resting on the dashboard. A crisp blue Yankee fitted sat ace-duce on his head, tickling the edge of his sunglasses. Though the lenses were completely black, Don B. saw it all through them. Pinched between his thick lips was a smoldering L of weed so strong that you could smell it down the block. It was only the finest of everything for Don B. When he noticed Ashanti, he said something to Tone before stepping out of the car to greet him.

Don B. extended hand. "What it do, my nigga?"

"Hanging and banging." Ashanti flapped the red bandana that was peeking from his right back pocket.

Don B. snickered as the gesture. "You guys are something else. Man, flaying colors went out years ago. All that shit does is point a bull's-eye on your back for the police and your enemies."

"All of my enemies are dead." Ashanti capped.

"And so are most of your friends, but what does that prove?" Don B. shot back. "Dig, I didn't call you out here to preach etiquette. I wanted to know if you down for getting some paper?"

"I'm always down to make some bread, depending on what it is?" Ashanti said.

Don B. laughed at his apprehension. "What's up, young blood? I thought you was a nigga down to do whatever whenever if the price was right?"

Now it was Ashanti's turn to laugh. "I am, but that don't mean I'm so eager to make a dollar that I'd run into some shit blindly. I know how you move, Don. If you coming to me then it means it a situation that your people can't handle. Don't beat me in the head. Come correct, Blood."

Don B. studied Ashanti for a few minutes before his lips spread into a wide grin. "You always were one of the sharper knives in the drawer. Take a walk with me right quick." Don B. placed his arm around Ashanti and led him around the corner. "Peep game, Ashanti. I'm having a little trouble with this producer nigga on my team. You remember Hollywood, right?"

Ashanti searched his mental database. "Yeah, the little light skinned nigga with the big mouth, right?"

"Yeah, that's the boy. I let him on the ship and now he's trying to rock the boat." Don B. told him.

Ashanti doubled over laughing. "I know you didn't call me all the way over here because Hollywood is giving you more trouble than you can handle. Don, that nigga is all bark and no bite. Slap the shit out of him and it'll straighten all this right out."

Don B. was irritated. "Ashanti, are you gonna be an asshole about this or listen to what I'm trying to tell you?"

"My fault. Go ahead, Don."

"Like I was saying, I let this nigga eat with me. After all his fraud bullshit from before I still brought him in and put some money in his pocket. I had Blood in the studio working on some tracks for me to throw on the next mix tape that a plan to shop for a side deal. I finally get these crackers at this record label interested and when it comes time to turn over the music, this nigga Hollywood pulls some funny shit."

"What did he do?" Ashanti was curious.

"The deal was he'd get half his bread up front and the other half when I got a label to sign off on the project. I managed to get a nice piece of change on the table for the group I'm trying to push so it was a win for everybody, or at least me and the artist. Of course I dressed it up to Hollywood like it was a small move to throw the nigga off, because we all know that the Don don't do small deals, right? Well, somebody must've put a bug in his ear that I was about to cake off from the project, because the next thing I know he's talking about renegotiating the terms. Now this is *Hollywood* we're talking about, so you know I'm not taking him seriously at first. I told him to go fuck himself and that the deal was going through regardless. That following Monday when I go see these dudes from the label to close on it, they inform me that they'd been contacted by Hollywood's lawyer with a claim that he wasn't properly compensated for his production work."

"Say word?" Ashanti was surprised. Hollywood had never been the smartest cat, but obviously he was smarter than a lot of them realized.

"Word is bond!" Don B. continued. "So, now I'm looking crazy to these dudes. They want the music, but not at the risk of ruining their reputation by being attached to a lawsuit. The only way for me to make the deal go through was to get Hollywood to sign off on the releases for the music."

Ashanti shrugged. "Don you know me. I'm an executioner, not an extortionist. Why didn't you just send some of your flunkies to pay a call on him?"

"I did. Tone sent some of the young boys over to holla at scrams. They gave him a nice beating, but that only made it worse. Instead of manning up and handling his business, dude takes out a restraining order against me. My nigga, the Hip-Hop tabloids are running crazy with this shit and that bitch ass nigga Hollywood is feeding them. They're calling me a gangster; can you believe this shit?"

"You, a gangster? Perish the thought." Ashanti said sarcastically.

"Word up. So now I'm not only caught up in this bum ass lawsuit, but I gotta clear this other shit up too. I'm looking crazy right now, B. I need something done about this in a hurry."

"This brings me back to my original question, why come to me?" Ashanti asked.

"I got a few cats I could've called on to handle this for me, but with all the heat on me behind this I can't risk having them fuck it up. I'm hot as a firecracker right now and I can't risk have this shit come back to me. I know if I get you on the case, it'll be clean."

"You want me to dead this dude?" Ashanti asked, ready to tell Don B. to go fuck himself.

"Nah, man. Why is your first thought always murder?" Don B. asked him.

Ashanti raised his eyebrow. "I told you, I'm an executioner. "

"I know, I know, but I need you to show some restraint with this. Dead is bad for business. I just need him to those releases so I can close on this deal. I know if anybody can persuade him, you can."

Ashanti thought on it for a minute. He knew Hollywood's character, fake ass baller who always let his mouth write checks his ass couldn't cash. He was harmless enough, but for some reason he seemed to have Don B. rattled. There was no doubt in Ashanti's mind that there was more to the story that Don B. wasn't telling, but he wouldn't press it.

"How much?" Ashanti asked.

Don B. couldn't hide the look of relief that came over his face. "You know the Don is gonna take care of you. Get ya man to sign these papers and I'll hit you with twenty-five hundred."

Ashanti gave Don B. a look. "Man, why you out here trying to play me, Blood?"

"What you talking about? Twenty-five hundred is good money." Don B. argued.

"Yeah, for one of these lil niggaz out here ready to short themselves just to get on your payroll." Ashanti countered. "I'll get homie to sign the papers, but it's gonna cost you five stacks."

Don B. looked at him as if he'd lost his mind. "See, now you trying to rob me."

"If I was trying to rob you, there'd be a gun in your mouth right now. I ain't a hard ass, Don B. All I want you to do is play fair."

"So, you think twenty-five hundred ain't fair? Dawg, you act like I'm asking you to kill him." Don B. said.

"No, but you want him to think you're willing to have him murdered, which is why you sought out a killer to approach him. Don B., I'm young but I ain't stupid. The fact that you set this meeting with me tells me I'm your last resort. If this situation is that serious you can dig in them deep ass pockets of yours and pay to make it disappear."

Don B. did his best to hide the irritation in his face. Ashanti was smarter than he gave him credit for, but he refused to concede so easily. "I don't know, fam. Five stacks is kinda steep for a shakedown. Maybe I should just go holla at one of my lil homies. I know a nigga that'll do it for a stack."

"Then go holla at that nigga and stop wasting my fucking time." Ashanti turned to walk away, but Don B. stopped him.

"Forever the ball buster, ain't you?" Don B. said with a sly grin. "A'ight, I'll give you your five stacks, shorty. Come by the office and pick it up when you take care of business."

Ashanti folded his arms. "Didn't we just establish the fact that I ain't a dummy? I need to see some paper up front."

"Ashanti, you ain't even done nothing yet and you expect me to pay you?"

"Indeed, I do. Before a lawyer sets foot in a courtroom they need a retainer. Same shit over here. Set that retainer out, my nigga." Ashanti slapped the back of his left hand into his right palm for emphasis.

Don B. was about to try and spin him but he could tell by the look on Ashanti's face that he would not be swayed. "Fucking thief." Don B. mumbled and dug into his pocket. He pulled out a stack of bills and counted threw them. He only had fifteen hundred in cash on him, which he handed to Ashanti.

Ashanti sifted through the bills and frowned. "See, now I feel like you're being disrespectful. I don't like to be disrespected." He absently adjusted the gun in his belt.

"Cool the fuck out. Nobody is trying to disrespect you, fam. That's all the bread I got on me. Handle this for me and come by to pick up the rest. I got you and you know the Don's word is good."

"I don't know about the Don's word, but I know about my word, so I'd advise you to listen real good to what I'm about to tell you. Shit is crazy in the hood right now, so all money down is not only appreciated, but needed. I'm gonna handle this thing for you, but make sure you come through on your end."

"I got you." Don B. promised. "But yo, for five stacks he better not only sign the paperwork, I also need you to send a real clear message as to what happens if you cross the Don."

"My message to him for crossing the Don will be as clear as my message to you if you cross *the Ashanti*." He imitated Don B's way of speaking of himself in third person. "I'll get word to you once the deed is done." Ashanti saluted him and headed down the block.

Don B. stood there on the corner of 124th and 7th watching Ashanti amble down the block with fifteen hundred dollars of his money in his pocket. Hollywood had been a thorn in his side that needed to be removed before the thorn became a knife. He could've gotten anyone to give Hollywood a beating, but he needed more than physical pain, he needed a psychological scar, which there was no doubt Ashanti would leave when it was all said and done. The young thug was just as sick and twisted as his mentor had been and he shuddered to think what method's Ashanti would use to persuade Hollywood. The papers would be signed, but it left Don B. wondering if in his solution he had potentially created a bigger problem.

"Fucking street niggaz." Don B. said to no one in particular and headed back to his car.

CHAPTER 6

When Diamonds stood to his full height he was bigger than Animal thought. He stood easily 6'3" with broad shoulders and a slender waist. A thick diamond flooded chain hung from around his neck. At the end of the chain was what looked like a shrunken head that had been dipped in white gold and sprinkled with black and white diamonds. The piece was so lifelike that it was almost grotesque. He stepped from around the table to greet them and when he smiled his teeth were encased in a diamonds and gold grill that was even more impressive than Animal's.

"So, this is the big bad wolf, eh?" Diamonds spoke with the hint of a French accent. "What it do, homie?"

"Maintaining." Animal said.

"Right, right. Listen, I heard about that lil scuff you got into earlier and just wanna apologize for being a poor host. I promised Sonja that I would take care of you while you were here." Diamonds said.

"I'm pretty good at taking care of myself, but thanks." Animal said.

Diamonds laughed. "So I've heard. Let me introduce you to my people." Diamonds turned to the table. "You already met, Blue." He nodded to the man with the patch over his eye. "That old hound dog has been with me since day one."

"And I'm gonna be with you until the last day." Blue said confidently.

Diamonds continued. "This my brother, Goldie." He patted the young man on the shoulder who had been sitting to his left.

The man introduced as Goldie looked like a young version of Diamonds, except with lighter skin and his dreads were dusty brown. He was wearing a white t-shirt with a black bandana tied snugly around his neck.

He nodded and raised his glass in Animal's direction, but didn't speak.

"Goldie don't talk much." Diamonds explained. "Me, Blue and Goldie came up from New Orleans when the government tried to wash it off the map and blame it on God. Had two more with us that didn't make it, but we've managed to find some pretty good replacements." Diamonds looked from Minister to the man with the cornrows. "The other quite one is my nigga, G." he was speaking of the man with the cornrows. "G is…"

"Leaving." G cut him off. Gathering his drink, he stood to leave the table. On the way past, G gave Animal a look and shook his head sadly.

"Fuck is his problem?" Animal glared at the parting man's back. He watched as G stopped to exchange a few words with the stripper named Reign before leaving the club.

Diamonds downplayed it. "Don't pay no mind to, G. You'd be bitter too if you ceased to exist, but I'm sure I ain't gotta explain disappearing acts to you, eh?" he winked. "G, don't much like anybody until he gets to know them. Once he rocks with you there's not a more solid cat that you'd wanna have at your side in a sticky situation."

"Down here they call him Teflon." Reign appeared seemingly out of thin air at Animal's side. She now had a thin robe covering her seminude body, but the sheer fabric did little to hide it.

"And why do they call him that?" Animal asked her. He didn't really care how G had gotten the nickname; he just wanted an excuse to address Reign directly.

"Because bullets can't kill him." Diamonds answered for her.

There was a look that passed between he and Reign that Animal picked up on, but acted as if he didn't notice.

"So now that you've met my lil family, let's get down to business." Diamonds continued. "Sonja says you need says you need to get to New York in a sho nuff hurry and some goodies to take with you for the ride, oui?"

Animal nodded. "Yeah, got some business I need to handle."

Diamonds nodded. "This what I hear. Sonja didn't get into what the business is, but I was hoping you could shed some light on it before we conducted any business."

Animal shrugged as if it was nothing. "Just something that I need to attend to."

"Youngster, you got a lot of nerve coming in here asking for our help but wanna be all secretive about what you got going on. For all we know you could be working with the police to bust us." Blue said.

Animal turned his attention to Blue. "No disrespect, but I didn't ask for your help, Sonja did. Furthermore, y'all know what it is with me, so never disrespect my pedigree by suggesting that I'm anything less than a gangster."

Diamonds laughed and clapped his hands thunderously. "I like this tadpole. He got some stones on him, don't he, Blue?"

"Either stones in his sack or rocks in his head." Blue said.

"Look, are y'all gonna help me or keep fucking with me? If you ain't gonna help, I can make my own way." Animal stood in frustration.

Diamonds' face became very serious. "Ain't no need to be disrespectful, friend. Let's not forget that you're still a guest in *my* house. Have a seat." He told Animal, but Animal remained standing. "Please." He added. Animal sat back down. "I think maybe we got off on the wrong foot here. Let's have a drink and everybody cool out."

Diamonds scanned the room until he spotted the waitress. She was near the stage taking the order of a kid wearing a red Dickey suit and heavy jewels. When she noticed Diamonds trying to get her attention she made to go to him, but the kid in the Dickey suit grabbed her by the arm. She pointed in Diamonds' direction and was trying to explain that she had to go, but guy didn't seem to care. He said something to his crew and nodded in Diamonds' direction which made them all laugh.

Diamonds was furious that his authority was being challenged in his domain. "Minister, go fetch that bitch." Minister nodded and walked across the room. He leaned in and started whispering something to the kid in the Dickey suit. "You see the shit I gotta put up with." Diamonds was speaking to Animal. "I'm up here trying to make a dollar and these Florida niggaz are more interested in making comedy movies. No offense." He said to Reign.

"None taken." She said in an easy tone.

A few seconds later, Minister came back with the waitress, who looked visibly shaken. "Sorry about that, Diamonds."

"We all good, baby girl. What was that all about?" Diamonds asked.

"Dude wants to run a tab, but he doesn't have a credit card. I tried to tell him that he had to pay for the drinks as he ordered them because he doesn't have a card and that's when he started getting all grabby, talking about how long his money is and how everybody in South Florida knows Flames."

Diamonds' looked over in Flames' direction. Flames stood up and spread his arms as if he was asking Diamonds what he was gonna do. "Go on and run him the tab, sweetie."

The waitress looked like she wanted to protest, but didn't. Animal watched her as she went back to the table where Flames was sitting to fill his order. While she was walking away, Flames slapped her on her ass and laughed with his friends. Animal didn't know him, but he couldn't stand him.

"Friend of yours?" Animal asked.

"Flames ain't a friend of nobody, but himself." Reign answered in disgust.

Diamonds kept his eyes on Flames, but spoke to Animal. "Flames was sort of the big man on campus when we came to Miami. He had all the shooters and all the best dope, until we showed up with what we had. That New Orleans dope was literally killing fiends and kept em coming back. We kept it to our lil slice of the city so as not to step on any toes, but eventually our competitions customers started coming to us. It didn't sit too well with Flames, with us lil country niggaz digging all into his pockets. Word is that he plans to make a move on us, but ain't tried nothing yet."

Animal was confused. "So, you know he's gonna make a move, yet you're sitting around and waiting for it instead of moving on him first?"

Diamonds laughed. "Outright killing Flames wouldn't go over too well with some of the locals. He has some very powerful friends that he makes a lot of money with and despite him being an asshole, keeping Flames breathing is in their best interests."

"Unless there was someone to take on his workload once he was gone." Reign added.

Diamonds shot her a look then turned back to Animal. "True, it'd make his death a bit easier to accept

117

if it didn't stop the money flow, but it ain't as easy as Reign is making it out to be. Flames ain't no pushover. He got a lot of guns and a lot of goons. Even if someone was lucky enough to get close enough to waste him, it'd still be a death sentence. At least for anyone *local*."

Animal didn't like the way Diamonds made the last statement. Animal raised his hand. "Let me stop you before you go any further. I don't know what Sonja told you, but my murder for hire days is over."

"Animal, don't bullshit me. You may not kill for money anymore, but you're still a killer. I smelled the blood on you the moment you stepped through the doors of Purple City. You give me this thing I want, and I'll give you what you want."

Animal's face twisted into a sneer. "Ain't this about a bitch? Sonja said I could trust you to help me, no strings attached, but you just like the rest. Nobody does something for nothing. Well fuck you and tell Red Sonja I said the same." Animal stood to leave.

"Gucci." When Diamonds spoke the name it froze Animal in his tracks. "I figured that would get your attention."

"What are you playing at, Diamonds?" Animal asked furiously.

"I ain't playing at nothing. I'm trying to strike a bargain. Please," he motioned for Animal to sit back down. He did. "Sonja's word is good and regardless of whether you kill Flames or not, I'm still gonna make sure you get what you need to handle your business. I'm just trying to sweeten the pot for all parties involved."

"I'm listening." Animal said.

Diamonds leaned in to whisper to him. "The tongue of my enemy will speak the name of the man who shot your girlfriend."

Animal was suspicious. "For all I know you could be bullshitting me. Just because you know Gucci got shot doesn't mean you know who did it. Everybody knows she got shot. It was on the news."

Diamonds grinned. "Yeah, but what the news didn't say was why she got shot. Your girlfriend got caught in the crossfire of some bullshit that didn't have nothing to do with her. What do they call it? A victim of circumstance."

Animal wanted to slap the smug grin of Diamonds' face but he didn't. A part of him wanted to get up and walk out to find his own way, but what if Diamonds did have the information he claimed to have?

Animal waved Diamonds off. "More shit you could've heard through the grapevine. You gotta come up with something better than that."

"I thought you might say as much." Diamonds reached under the table and produced something wrapped in plastic, which he slid across the table to Animal. Animal eyed the plastic suspiciously. "It ain't gonna bite, but it may sting you a bit emotionally."

With trembling hands, Animal unwrapped the plastic. Inside there was some kid of green fabric. Slowly he pulled it out and held it in front of him. It was made of a soft material that was caked with dark brown liquid. Animal had seen enough blood to know it on sight. When Animal held it up to fully examine it, he felt all the air rush from his body. It was a green dress. The same green dress he'd brought for Gucci right before his arrest. He remembered it because she kept hinting around to how much she'd liked it when they were in the store. Animal acted like he wasn't paying attention, but he doubled back and bought it for her the next day. She was supposed to wear it on their next date night, but he was taken away from her before he could see it on her.

Animal buried his face in the dress and inhaled deep. It had been years, but he would know her scent anywhere. "Gucci." He sobbed into the dress.

"She was wearing it the night they put a hole in her." Diamonds said. He hadn't meant to be so insensitive with his statement; it just came out that way.

With a roar Animal sprang to his feet and flipped the table over. He snatched Diamonds to his feet by the front of his shirt and rained spittle in his face when he roared. "Who did it? Tell me who shot my lady and they're dead. Their mothers, fathers, brothers and sisters. I will put them all in the ground. Tell me, Diamonds!" Animal demanded.

Everyone at the table was instantly in motion, drawing weapons, but not Diamonds. He smiled at the enraged young man as if they were having a light conversation. "There is no doubt in my mind that the body count in New York is gonna jump when you touch the town, mon ami, but first thing's first. Let's start with you taking your hands off me before my people get the wrong idea about your intentions."

For the first time Animal noticed that he was surrounded and everybody had a gun pointed at him. Even Unique stood nervously to the side with her blade in hand. Animal wanted to tear into them all, but he couldn't blame them. They were doing what they were supposed to be doing, which was protecting their king. With a sigh, he released Diamonds.

"I'm sorry." Animal lowered his head.

Diamonds placed a hand on Animal's shoulder. "Ain't no apologies necessary. Grief make a man's brains all scrambled and its obvious that you're grieving something awful. Animal, let me tell you something I learned a long time ago about this business we're in. We who pay the game do so with a clear understanding of what we're getting into, but civilians are innocent. You will have your vengeance on the one who did this, but the name you seek comes at a price. You willing to pay it?"

Animal simply nodded because he didn't trust his words in such an emotional state.

"Good. Now when you do it, I need it to be clean. I can't have anything that will lead back to me, do you understand?" Diamonds asked.

Animal's voice was hard and cold when he replied. "When I kill a man, you can always expect it to be clean, but for the name of the dude who tried to waste my old lady," he shook his head. "His mama is going to have to lay him to rest in a sippy cup, because there won't be enough left of him for a coffin."

And with that, the bargain was struck.

CHAPTER 7

Hollywood was a man who could best be described as a man with champagne dreams with forty-ounce ambition. He was born and raised on the rough streets of Harlem, but while his friends were finding ways out through drugs, sports or music, Hollywood found his way out through the art of manipulation.

Hollywood wasn't the toughest cat on the block, but he could talk you into thinking that he was. That was his gift, the ability to make people believe what wasn't. This was how he got his start and what would eventually be his undoing.

For as long as Hollywood could remember, he wanted to be a rapper. Day and night, he would write rhymes that he would perform in front of the bathroom mirror or for his friends in the hood., His lyrics sucked but the yes-men he kept around him convinced

125

Hollywood that he had the golden touch. As he got older and the window of opportunity began to close for the young rapper, Hollywood switched hats and decided he wanted to be a producer/record executive. He assembled some fierce young crew of rappers and producers and got them all to believe in his version of the American dream. Hollywood capitalized off the talent around him and was able to make a few power moves, most of which he reaped the benefit from. Word was out that there was a kid name Hollywood from out of Harlem who had some dope beats for lease or sale, which is what brought him to the attention of the Big Dawg C.E.O. Don B.

Hollywood agreed to sell Don B. some beats for some projects that he had going on, but what he didn't tell Don B. was that he was not the true composer of the beats. This would come out later. Hollywood had made some nice money off Big Dawg entertainment

126

until one of his disgruntle young producers exposed him. When Don B. had gotten wise to the ruse he had Hollywood beaten and embarrassed in front of the whole Big Dawg staff. Hollywood hope that would be the end of it, but he was still in debt to Don B. and the Don wanted his money. With no way to pay him back Hollywood became an indentured servant at Big Dawg. Don B. kept him literally chained up in the studio, working around the clock.

Spending so much time in the high-tech studio Hollywood eventually became good at actually producing songs. He was still property of Big Dawg Entertainment, but Don B. was letting him keep some of the money he kept from making beats, taxing him heavily and applying the money to what Hollywood owed. It was an unfair relationship and at times embarrassing, but Hollywood didn't care. The only thing that mattered to him was that he was finally *on*, no matter how it happened.

Don B. had Hollywood working slave hours on various projects which gave him free run of the studio and time to plot a way to manipulate the situation to work to his advantage. At first, he was just going to sneak off like a thief in the night, taking all of his work and then some with him, but when he'd gotten word of Don B's pending deal he had a better idea.

Hollywood wished that the could've seen the look on Don B's face when he found out that his little deal had been stalled because of the lawsuit filed against Big Dawg Entertainment. He might not have gotten a chance to see Don B's facial expression, but the fact that he was pissed was made apparent when three of Big Dawg's henchmen caught him coming out of the club one night and beat the dog shit out of him. They'd blackened both of Hollywood's eyes and fractured his ankle so he would be on a cane for the next few weeks. Hollywood was going to chuck it up and accept his beating like a man, until his baby's mother put the idea in his head to press charges and extort Don B. to drop them. He didn't like the idea, but he did it anyway and it only succeeded in making him more of an outcast. Now, not only was a sucker for the way he let Big Dawg treat him all those years, but he was now branded a snitch too.

Hollywood was a marked man who had been living in hiding in his apartment for the last two weeks. Most of the time if he needed something from outside he would send his baby's mother, but if he had to go himself, he never left the house without his friend Melvin who he had hired as a bodyguard. Of course, Hollywood didn't have the money to pay him, but he sold Melvin on the idea that he would be taken care of when the lawsuit money came in. Hollywood planned to vanish without a trace and stiff Melvin once he got paid, but little did he know, Melvin had idea of his own. He glued himself to Hollywood's side so that when the money finally did start coming in, he could rob him blind. They made the perfect pair because they were two snakes in a pod.

Hollywood sat hunched over his computer, rolling his finger back and forth over the mouse pad. He had been tweaking the beat he was working on for the past four hours, but something about it still sounded off. He reached over and grabbed his pack of cigarettes off the table. When he went to pluck one out, he noticed that the pack was empty.

Hollywood crumbled the pack of cigarettes and tossed them into the trash can. "Fuck. Yo, let me get a cigarette." He told Melvin.

Melvin patted his pockets and shrugged. "I ain't got no more. I was smoking yours."

"I guess that explains why I ain't got none." Hollywood said with an attitude. "Let's go to the corner store and get some more." Using the help of his cane, he got up from the chair and limped out the door with Melvin on his heels.

Melvin walked a head, while Hollywood trailed a few paces behind. He carefully checked both stairwells before waving Hollywood forward to the elevator.

"So how long you think it's gonna be before that bread comes in?" Melvin asked.

Hollywood sucked his teeth. "My dude, how many times are you gonna ask me about that money?"

"I ain't trying to be all on your back about it, Hollywood. It's just that I know these lawsuits can take a long time and bills are piling up at my crib." Melvin told him.

"Mel, I keep telling you that we gonna get paid in a few weeks. Don B. doesn't want this to go to court because I got him by the balls. He's gonna settle, my lawyer told me as much." Hollywood lied. What the lawyer had actually told him was that Don B. was fighting the suit tooth and nail and there was no way to know for sure when a settlement would be reached.

"A'ight, man. I'm just itching to get a few dollars in my pocket." Melvin pressed for the elevator.

"I know. I got you my nigga." Hollywood told him.

When the elevator door slid open, everything seemed to move in slow motion. Hollywood's brain registered that there was someone standing in the elevator, holding something in his hand, but it didn't send the signal to his mouth fast enough to warn Melvin. Ashanti struck Melvin in the chest with the cattle prod, sending ten thousand volts into his heart. Melvin staggered, eyes wide with shock, trying to figure out what was going on. Ashanti hit him again, this time in his head, dropping Melvin to the ground.

The big man lay on the dirty hallways floor, twitching, with drool running out of the side of his mouth.

Hollywood hobbled off back down the hall towards his apartment as fast as he could, but with his fractured ankle there was no way for him to out run Ashanti. Ashanti tapped the cattle prod against Hollywood's ass, drawing a high-pitched squeal. He stumbled forward, but managed to keep his footing with the help of his cane. Realizing that he couldn't outrun his attacker, Hollywood decided to try and fight. He turned around and swung his cane at Ashanti's head, but Ashanti blocked it with the cattle prod and followed with a right hook to Hollywood's jaw. Hollywood fell to the ground, landing on his stomach and tried to crawl away.

Ashanti poked Hollywood in the ass once more with the cattle prod, causing him to flail around on the ground like a fish. "Man, why don't you stay your ass still before I end up barbecuing your briefs with this shit."

Hollywood threw his hands up defensively. "A'ight, a'ight. Just chill with that thing. What you want from me?"

Ashanti pulled the release forms from his pocket and held them out for Hollywood to see. "Not much. Just need your signature on these and I'll be on my way."

Hollywood immediately recognized the paperwork. "Nah, man. I told Don B. I ain't letting him jerk me no more."

"I don't think you have much of a choice. Sign the papers before you make me do something I regret." Ashanti said.

"I ain't signing nothing. What are you gonna do, kill me? If I'm dead, the papers will never get singed and

Don B. will still be fucked." Hollywood said, thinking
he had figured a way to worm his way out of it.

Ashanti shook his head. "Have it your way. By the
time it's all said and done two things are gonna happen,
you're gonna assign these papers and you're gonna
learn that there are some things worse than death."
Ashanti grabbed Hollywood by his shirt and dragged
him towards his apartment.

Hollywood was in a bad way and he knew it, even
before Ashanti shoved him into the bathroom and
produced a roll of duct tape. Ashanti had bound him to
one of the kitchen chairs and sat him in the bathtub,
which was filled ankle high with water. From the

mischievous grin on his face he knew that the youngster had something sinister planned for him.

Ashanti sat on the edge of the bathtub. He had the cattle prod in his hand, which was now covered in a dish glove that he'd found under the sink. He regarded Hollywood. "See, we could've done this simple, but you wanted to be a hard ass about it. We'll do it your way. You gonna sign the papers?"

"Listen, it ain't gotta be like this. I got some bread coming to me real soon from this lawsuit. Whatever Don B. is paying you, I'll double it." Hollywood tried to barter.

"Wrong answer." Ashanti touched the water with the end of the cattle prod. Hollywood shook violently in the char as sparks leapt from the water around his feet.

"Oh my God. Please stop." Hollywood pleaded.

"I'll stop as soon as you sign the release forms." Ashanti told him.

"You don't understand, man. This nigga Don B. has been jerking me for years over this music. He keeps me chained up in the studio working damn near around the clock for free. My girl had to go on welfare just so we could feed our kids." Hollywood tried to appeal to Ashanti's sense of humanity.

"Not my problem." Ashanti touched the cattle prod to the water and gave him another shock.

Hollywood's whole body tingled. His fingers and toes were numb and he was lightheaded. He was about to make another futile attempt for his life when someone appeared in the bathroom doorway, startling both of them.

"What the fuck is this?" Hollywood's baby's mother stood on the door way watching the strange sight before her. She was a pretty girl with fair skin and long hair, which she wore in a ponytail that day.

"Baby, run!" Hollywood shouted.

His baby's mother turned and tried to bolt, but Ashanti pulled her back into the bathroom by her ponytail. "Wrong place, wrong time, shorty." Ashanti threw her against the sink.

To her credit, Hollywood's baby's mother had more heart than he did. She came at Ashanti throwing a series of combinations that caught him off guard. She managed to land a lucky shot to the lip, drawing blood. Ashanti spat the blood into the murky tub and glared at her. "You know you fucked up, right?"

Hollywood's baby's mother came back at Ashanti, but this time he was prepared. She threw wild punches which he easily swatted and gave her a strong hook to the gut. She folded like a sack of potatoes at his feet.

"If you touch her, I swear to God I'll kill you!" Hollywood struggled against his restraints.

"Shut you bitch ass up." Ashanti dipped the cattle prod into the water. This time he left it in long enough for Hollywood to get a good taste of the voltage. In the midst of his torture session, he had an idea. He rested on the tub and pulled the semiconscious girl onto his lap. He stroked the side of her cheek. "Your lady ain't bad looking, man." He taunted Hollywood.

The look in Ashanti's eyes and the intimacy of his touch filled Hollywood's mind with thoughts of the worse. "See, you going too far. This is between us. She ain't got nothing to do with it."

"She has everything to do with it. Guilt by association, play boy." Ashanti told him. "Now, you can either sign these papers or I'm gonna let you watch me fuck this fine bitch in every hole in her body, before I kill the both of you."

Hollywood weighed his options. He knew that if he signed the papers then all was lost and he would be left with nothing, but if he didn't sign, only God knew what would happen to his baby's mother. A part of him wondered what life would be like without her nagging ass, and he was almost tempted to hold out. Truth be told, Hollywood loved her, even if it was in his own twisted way, and he wasn't willing to risk her. "I'll sign." He said just above a whisper.

Ashanti plunged the cattle prod into the water. "I didn't hear you mutha fucka!" he shouted over Hollywood's screams.

"I said I'll sign. Just please stop." Hollywood gasped.

Ashanti retrieved the papers and placed them on the side of the tub, careful not to get them wet. He cut one of Hollywood's arms free and placed a pen in his hand.

Hollywood had a murderous look in his eyes and his grip tightened around the pen.

Ashanti smiled. "You're welcome to try it, but you better be damn sure." Hollywood wisely abandoned the heroics he had planned and signed the papers. "Now that was painless." Ashanti tucked the papers back into his pocket.

"You got what you want. Now get the fuck outta my house!" Hollywood snapped.

"Sure thing, tough guy." Ashanti grabbed Hollywood's baby's mother and shoved her into the tub with her man. The water woke her up with a start and her eyes narrowed to slits when they landed on Ashanti. "I'm gonna leave you two love birds to it, but before I do, I wanna do my part to help bring the spark back into y'all relationship." Ashanti tossed the cattle prod into the tub.

Both Hollywood and his baby's mother shrieked as the prod broke the surface of the water. They expected to die excruciating deaths, but the rod sank harmlessly to the bottom of the tub. The couple looked up at Ashanti with confused expressions.

"It's gotta be on to generate a charge and I turned it off before I tossed it in." Ashanti answered the unspoken question. "I'm a criminal, not a monster." He told them before slipping out of the apartment.

Ashanti waited until he was outside before letting go the laugh he'd been holding for the passed ten minutes. Hollywood was a pussy that Don B. shouldn't have had to call him to handle, but he wasn't mad that he did. He would be five thousand dollars richer for a few minutes of work. The best part was that he didn't have to kill anybody to get the job done. He was growing up. Ashanti beamed because he knew that if Animal had been there to see him in action he'd be proud.

CHAPTER 8

Normally Animal would've stalked the victim for at least a week before moving on him, but he didn't have that kind of time. He needed to get back to Gucci ASAP, so he kept it to three days; two to get a feel for Flames' movements and one to push him off the planet.

Because of the incident with the sneaky valet it was deemed best if Animal abandoned his hotel room. His identification and method of payment had both been fakes and the few pieces of clothing he had left behind wouldn't be missed, so there was nothing tying him to the room. Diamonds had set him up in an apartment out by the airport that he usually reserved for his jump-offs. It was small, but neat and more than enough space for Animal. He didn't plan on being there any longer than he had to.

Animal didn't know Miami so he needed a guide. He had expected it to be Minister, but was pleasantly surprised when Reign showed up one early morning. She'd abandoned the purple wig and contacts, so for the first time Animal saw the face behind the mask. Reign was pretty girl, who looked far younger than she had with her face caked in makeup the first night he'd met her. Reign's real hair was twisted into neat black locks which she wore braided into a thick bun at the back of her head. She was dressed in a pair of blue denim shorts that were so tight they looked like underwear and a pink baby doll tank top that read *Born 2 Ride*. Her thick nipples pressed against the fabric without the restraint of a bra. Animal tried not to look, but he couldn't help himself.

Picking up on his distraction, Reign placed one hand at the top of the doorway so the tank top hugged her breast a little tighter. "So, you just gonna stand there looking at my tits or let me in?"

From the moment Animal invited Reign across the threshold he knew she was going to be trouble, but he liked living on the edge.

The first order of business was to get a line on Flames which proved to be easier than Animal would've thought. It seemed that everyone in South Florida indeed knew Flames. Finding him was one thing, but getting to him would be another. He moved carefully and rolled with a ruthless gang of young boys under him, who all loved to commit murder. They were with him almost twenty-four seven. Animal was ready to just run up on him and gun it out, but Reign had a better idea.

Flames had homes all throughout South Florida that he used for various things, but his best kept secret was a townhouse just outside Coco Beach, which Reign just happened to track down the address to. On the second day of their surveillance Reign took Animal to a small apartment that was located a few blocks from where Flames' place was. When Animal asked her how she was able to get an apartment so conveniently close to Flames' place on such short notice she simply said "It belongs to a friend of mine." He didn't believe her. Animal could tell from the time he'd met her that there was more to Reign that met the eye, and he intended to find out what it was before he made her his co-defendant on a murder case.

That night Animal and Reign lounged in the apartment, laying their final plans. It was hotter than the devil outside so Reign was wearing a pair of shorts and a bikini top. She sat in a chair, legs spread, letting the fan cool her off. With Reign, gestures as simple as fixing her hair seemed seductive and Animal found himself staring at her even when he didn't want to.

Watching Reign was a distraction so to take his mind off it Animal busied himself cleaning the guns Diamonds had provided for them.

"I think those guns are about clean enough, don't you?" Reign asked.

"You can never be too careful." Animal said, not bothering to take his eyes off the guns.

"Can I ask you something?"

"Sure." He said.

"How come you never look at me?"

Animal was confused. "What do you mean? I look at you all the time."

"Yeah, but that's mostly when you think I'm not looking. I mean, how come you don't *look* at me? It's as if you're afraid to make eye contact." Reign explained.

"I ain't afraid of nothing." Animal boasted.

"So, I'm told. That only leaves me to wonder why you get so nervous around lil old me?" Reign got up from the chair and came to stand before Animal.

His eyes traveled from her flat stomach to her playful eyes. "Reign, you tripping." Animal got up to walk away, but she blocked his path.

She moved closer to him and invaded his space. "I don't think I am. Most men can't take their eyes off me, but not you."

"I learned a long time ago not to ogle things that don't belong to me." Animal said.

"Reign belongs to no one." She shot back.

"What about Diamonds?"

Reign laughed. "Diamonds is my business partner and my comrade. Have I fucked him? Sure, I fucked a lot of niggaz, but I don't belong to Diamonds. I'm a free agent." She reached out to touch Animal's face, but he backed away.

Reign closed the distance between them.

"Too bad I'm not." Animal backed up, but she kept coming. Eventually she forced his back against the wall. Reign was standing so close that he could smell the remnants of turkey from the sandwich she'd had earlier.

"Who're you talking about, Gucci or Sonja?" Reign smiled as the look of surprise registered on Animal's face. "Don't look so shocked, boo. I deal in information, amongst other things." She touched his chest.

Animal grabbed her by the wrist. "Don't."

"Don't what? Make you feel good?" she laid her other hand on his chest. "When is the last time you've been shown the kindness of a woman?"

"There's only one woman's kindness I'm interested in." Animal told her, but he didn't make an attempt to move her hand. Feeling the heat from her palm spread a warmth through him that pooled somewhere in his groin.

Reign leaned in and whispered in Animal's ear. "That little broken angel in New York can have your heart. I'm interested in the simpler things." She ran her hand over his dick, which was rock hard in his shorts.

Animal moved to push Reign away, but she spun with his weight and took his legs out from under him. They ended up crashing to the floor with Reign on top of him. She looked her legs around his and bent one arm behind Animal's head. He tried to use his other one to push her off, but she had him at an awkward angel and it was hard for him to get the leverage.

"Stop playing with me, Reign." Animal said in a threatening tone.

"Who is playing? Nigga, you come down here talking that distraught lover shit, when I know you're fresh out the next bitch's pussy." Reign said.

"You don't know what you're talking about." Animal told her.

"I told you, I deal in information. I heard all the little nasty stories about you and Red Sonja. I'll bet that warm Latina mouth helped keep your mind off poor old Gucci plenty of nights." She licked his chin.

Animal bucked and managed to toss Reign off of him. He rolled over on her and wrapped his hand around his throat. He had a fire burning in his eyes that danced somewhere between hate and lust. Reign just looked up at him with playful eyes and laughed.

"You must've heard that I like it rough!" Reign grabbed Animal by the back of his hair and yanked so hard that his neck cracked. With his hand free of her throat, Reign slid between his legs and came up behind him. Animal was in a kneeling position and when he tried to get up, she kicked his leg out from under him so he dropped back on his knees. Before he could react, Reign came around front and wrapped her legs around his neck, straddling his chin.

"Reign, you better stop fucking around before I…" Animal was cut off when she tightened her grip around his neck.

"Before what? Before you decide to stop lying to yourself and feed that monster clawing at your back right now. You smell this good shit here?" Reign moaned, grinding her pussy against his face.

Reign's scent made Animal dizzy and his control was slipping fast. A part of him wanted to bite a hole in the skimpy shorts and taste her, but wouldn't be manipulated. Animal cupped Reigns ass and got to his feet, with her still attached firmly to his neck. He ripped her free and slammed her to the bed roughly. He had a maddened look in his eyes when he jumped on the bed after her.

"You wanna play games, little bitch? I'll show you how I play!" Animal tore her bikini top off. Reign's breasts were plump and stood firmly, with dark chocolate nipples peeking at him accusingly.

Reign licked her fingers and began playing with her nipples. "That's right, baby. Show me that boogey man that I keep hearing about. Take this pussy."

Animal dove on her and ravaged her breasts. He gave each nipple equal attention as he traced circles around them with her tongue. Beneath him, Reign slipped out of her panties and shorts. With her free hand she snatched his belt off and slid his shorts down over his lips. Animal's dick burst free like a roaring elephant trunk. Reign jerked his dick, using her thumb to smear pre-cum over the head as it leaked out.

"Let me taste that." Reign slid from beneath him and laid Animal on his back. She spit on his dick, rubbing her saliva up and down his shaft to get it nice and slick before she attacked it. Reign jackknifed Animal's dick in and out of her throat, occasionally making gagging sounds. She was rough with the dick but that balance of pleasure and pain turned him on.

Animal grabbed a hand full of Reign's locks as she sucked him to new heights. He forced her head down further, but instead of pulling away she went with it. She let Animal fuck her so deep in her throat that he could've sworn his dick brushed against her tonsils. She started sucking him at an angle, moving her head from side to side and brining him closer to a climax. Animal howled like a wounded dog and exploded in Reign's mouth. She continued to suck him, making sure she got out every drop and then some, while he lay there with his leg shaking.

Animal had never cum so hard in his life. He looked over at the silent television screen mounted on the wall and saw the scene that had just unfolded in the glass' reflection. He laid there, chest heaving and spent. Reign had slowed her sucking to a suckle, working to keep him erect. Animal suddenly felt like shit on a stick. He had come to Miami with a purpose and let his dick sidetrack him. He had betrayed Gucci…again.

"Chill out, baby girl." Animal pushed Reign off him gently and got off the bed.

She watched him fixing his shorts with a look of confusion on her face. "Where you going? I just about had ya man ready for round two." Reign got off the bed and moved to put her arms around Animal, but he stopped her.

"I said chill."

"I can dig it. You need a few minutes to recover? A'ight, I'm about to roll up and when can finish what we started." Reign said.

"Nah, I don't think that would be a good idea. We should've never gone there, Reign. It was a mistake." Animal told her.

Reign gave him a look. "A mistake? No-the-fuck you didn't. I didn't hear you talking about no mistakes when you were blowing your load in my mouth, nigga!" she was furious.

"Reign, I ain't trying to argue with you and I sure as hell ain't trying to blame you. All I'm saying is that we both know what it is and why I'm here, so going there would only complicate shit." He said sincerely.

Reign folded her arms and tapped her foot. "You New York niggaz kill me the way y'all think you can take what you want and not be held accountable. It ain't the fact that you don't wanna get involved with me that's got me tight. That's a blessing because you got too many issues for a bitch to deal with. I'm just tripping on the fact that you don't even have the common decency to let me get my nut after you got yours. That's some crab shit."

"You're right, and I'm sorry, Reign." Animal was trying to defuse the argument by conceding.

"I'll fucking bet. I know your type, Animal. I see niggaz like you come in and out the club every night, but you're a master at your bullshit. You sing this sad ass tale of woe and being ready to die for love, but that's how you get chicks to let their guards down. As soon as a bitch is all wrapped up in your cause, you get what you need and leave them high and dry. I know how that's how it played out with Sonja and it's what you're doing to me right now. You probably did the same shit to ol' girl in New York and now guilt got you running back trying to play Captain-Save-A-Ho."

"Fuck you, Reign. You don't know shit about me." Animal stormed towards the door.

"I know more about you than you think and that's why your ass is mad now!" She threw the fan at the door. It slammed closed just before the fan shattered against it.

CHAPTER 9

After what had happened at the apartment with Reign the working relationship between her and Animal had become compromised, so he had to go the rest of the way alone. He returned to the place Diamonds had provided for him and laid his plans for the final phase of Flames' murder. When he didn't return to the apartment that night, Diamonds put out an A.P.B for him. Animal knew it was more out of wanting to know if he was going to finish the job rather than him being okay. When Animal and Diamonds finally spoke, he assured him that the job would be handled. He didn't know if Reign had told him about what transpired between them and he didn't stay on the phone with him long enough for Diamonds to bring it up.

On the third night Animal made careful preparations for his hit on Flames. He no longer had the convenience of the apartment down the street, but he didn't need it. He had watched Flames long enough to where he got a pretty good idea of his routines...at least he hoped so. Animal didn't like to rush when it came to murder, but he didn't have much a choice. The longer he waited the more he ran the risk of being sidetracked again. He wanted to finish Flames off and get out of Miami and back to the business of revenge.

Going at it alone only made things more difficult, but Animal was used to that. He was at his best when he worked alone. Up to that point he had making slow progress by staying one step behind Flames, but that wouldn't get the job done, so Animal decided move one step ahead of him.

It had been a good night for Flames, even for a Monday. It was his homie Rob's birthday and they decided to celebrate in high style at King of Diamonds, which was a prominent gentleman's club in Miami.

They had popped bottles and made it rain all night long, drawing the attentions of all the strippers and the animosities of the dudes who were ignored by the girls in favor of Flames and his entourage. Flames was a regular so he had run through a bunch of the girls who worked there, but there was one nut he had yet to crack.

She was a fine young thing from Orlando, FL who had a slick mouth and a phat ass. She danced under the name Jade, but Flames had found out that her government name was Janette. In just over a month of working at K.O.D., she had managed to run afoul of most of the girls and gain the favor of some of its heaviest spenders. She was about her paper and didn't care whose toes she stepped on to get it, which is what turned Flames on the most about her.

Janette's name had been attached to some notable street cats the Florida area, but none more so than her son's father, Gator. Flames had never met him personally, but his story was the stuff of legends in every hood.

They called Gator one of the last fallen legends because of the way he had gone out, guns blazing and bodies dropping. Too bad the bodies were those of police officers. He took four of theirs before he was eventually cut down. Word had it wasn't the police's bullets that killed him, but the beating that followed on the way to the hospital. He had murdered several police officers and prison wasn't an option for a cop killer. The officer's made sure they paid special attention to his face so that his family couldn't have an open casket funeral. Janette got by as best she could at first off of her baby's father's reputation, but it eventually got old and she had to find a real way to support her and her son, Nickels. With little to no skills, she turned to the only other thing that she had of value, her body. Packing her son up, she took her show on the road and eventually ended up in Miami.

That night luck must've been on Flames' side because Janette had given him some rhythm. He promised her a few dollars and night she wouldn't forget it she agreed to leave the club with him for a *special* after party. When Janette saw the bankroll he was carrying, that sealed the deal. Shortly before closing time, Janette left King of Diamonds with Flames and his entourage.

Flames ditched the rest of his crew and slid off with Rob, Janette and one of the other strippers. Flames was in his truck with Janette, while Rob followed in his Mercedes with the other stripper. The plan was to dip out to Flames' townhouse in Coco Beach and keep the party going. They already had bottles and weed, but as it turned out the girls wanted to snort a little. Flames was drunk and horny so there was no way he was making the detour, so Rob and the other stripper went to score, while Flames and Janette kept going to the house, and they'd meet up later.

Flames had barely gotten his key in the door before he and Janette were all over each other. Flames grabbed Janette by the back of her head and kissed her passionately. Janette had been in the club fucking and sucking all night, but it wasn't even a second thought in Flames' drunken brain. Flames and the girl staggered through the front door and into the living room, pawing, kissing and trying to tear each other's clothes off. They were so caught up in each other that neither of them initially noticed that someone was in the house. There intense lip-lock was broken when they heard the familiar sound of a gun being cocked.

Animal's voice cut the darkness. "Had I known you were brining company home, I'd have set an extra place at the table."

Flames was stunned. Never in a million years would he have thought he could be ambushed in his townhouse. It was like his safe haven, and he had taken every precaution to keep it that way, but the man sitting in his living room proved that he hadn't been careful enough. There were only a few people who knew about the townhouse and Flames started ticking off the names in his head.

Flames knew that any minute, Rob would be back from scoring the coke and this little party would come to an abrupt end, but when he was coming was anyone's guess. Flames hoped it wasn't one of those nights when Rob decided he couldn't wait and fucked the girl in the car, because at that point he was his only hope. Flames needed time, so he tried to stall.

"From yo accent I can tell you ain't from round here, so you can't possibly know who it is you trying to rob, dawg. I'm holding the biggest bag in this whole city." Flames said in his toughest tone.

Animal leaned forward, resting his elbows on his knees. The gun dangled causally between his legs. "If only it was as simple as a robbery. You, my friend," he was pointing the gun at Flames for emphasis as he spoke, "hold the key to something I crave more than money."

"And what's that?" Flames asked and immediately regretted the question.

"Revenge." Animal let the hammer rock.

The first shot skipped off Flames' forehead, taking pieces of his skull with it and painting rich splatter pattern on the wall behind him. The second shot caved Flames' chest in and knocked him off his feet. His body landed a few feet away from the terrified Janette. When she laid eyes on her would-be benefactor's face, she felt ill. What was left of his ruined mouth flapped open and closed like a beached fish, as he whimpered something that was too distorted for her to make out.

Janette snapped and opened her mouth to scream for help, but Animal's hand around her neck trapped the scream in her throat. "You'll get your chance to scream," he kissed her on the lips softly, "but you'll have to wait your turn." He slapped her viciously across the face, knocking her out.

With the girl out of the way, Animal was free to focus on Flames. He lay slumped in the middle of the floor, looking less like the *big man on campus* and more like the *dead nigga on the living room floor.* He had to give his adversary credit. Flames was good, but when it was all said and done, Animal was better.

After checking Flames' pulse to make sure he was dead, Animal disappeared into the kitchen and came back out a few seconds, holding a paring knife that looked like it had never been used. He knelt over Flames, trying not to focus on the dead eyes staring up at him. Animal had never been on to desecrate the dead, but Diamonds had been specific in his terms, so Animal would be specific in his delivery.

Animal pried Flames dead mouth open and pinched the corpse's tongue between his fingers. "As I'm told, your tongue will speak the name of the man I'm looking for. Let's see what you have to say."

Janette was awakened by what felt like someone licking her face. She turned her head in the direction of the tongue and began to suckle it gently between her lips. Slowly the fog began to roll back from her brain and remembering where she was, her eyes snapped open with a start. She was greeted by Animal's grinning face hovering over hers. Pinched between his fingers playfully was a severed tongue. It didn't take a rocket scientist to know whose it was.

"Oh my God." She recoiled and scrambled into the corner.

Animal stood and stalked slowly towards her. "Nah, not God, more like the rebellious little brother who they kicked outta heaven. I think you know who I mean." Animal drew his gun and chambered a round.

"Please don't kill me," she pleaded.

"No loose ends, baby. It's one of the first lessons I learned and a rule I live by." Animal pointed the gun at her.

"But I got a kid." She said, tears pouring down her cheeks.

"Good." Animal nodded. "That means they'll be somebody to mourn your passing," he told her before blowing her brains out.

With Flames tongue wrapped in a strip of cloth and tucked in his pockets, Animal's work was done and it was time for him to make his exit. He stopped short of the door and took a minute to admire the mess he'd made. When his eyes landed on Janette's corpse, he found that he couldn't. In the morning a child would wake up crying for its mother, but mommy wouldn't be coming home. Not that morning, not ever. Animal studied her face. He tried to imagine her story and stir some sort of remorse within himself but he felt none.

She was a whore who had made the mistake of trying to turn the wrong trick that night. Someone would mourn her, but it wouldn't be Animal. He crossed himself and slipped from the apartment.

Animal made hurried steps down the block, tugging at his hoodie to make sure his face remained obscured. The street was empty, save for a man walking his Doberman. The dog growled at the approaching youth, but the man pulled it by the leash and crossed the street. When Animal bent the corner, a green Mercedes was coming his way. He had to cover his eyes against the glare of the headlights. As the car passed Animal and the driver made eye contact. The driver's eyes pause on Animal as if he was trying to place him, but Animal disappeared into the night before he could make a positive I.D.

Rob and the stripper pulled up in Flames' driveway and parked behind his truck. They got out of the car, falling all over each other. They were clearly drunk and it was a wonder they hadn't gotten a D.U.I. Rob steered the stripper up the cobblestone walk way to the front door of the townhouse. He went to knock on the door and noticed that it was partially open. For as paranoid as Flames was, it wasn't like him to leave his door open. Rob's instincts went off and he was instantly sober. He drew his gun and entered the apartment with the stripper on his heels. She was firing off questions at a million miles per minute, but Rob ignored her, instead paying attention to the shadows dancing around Flames' living room.

Rob noticed something on the wall and moved closer to investigate. Cautiously he ran his fingers over the stain and felt that it was wet. Upon closer inspection he realized that it was blood. Rob stumbled backward in shock, sweeping his gun back and forth across the dark living room.

"What's going on?" the stripper asked.

"I don't know. Hit that light on the wall." Rob told her.

The stripper felt her way along the wall until she felt switches. She flicked all three of them at the same time and the living room was bathed in light, temporarily blinding Rob and the stripper. Her vision cleared first, and when she took stock of the scene in the living room she let out a scream. Rob covered his mouth in shock and backed up to the wall. Sprawled on the living room floor were Flames and Janette.

"Fuck, fuck, fuck!" Rob paced the living room. It had only been fifteen minutes or so since Rob had left Flames to get the coke and came back, so the killer couldn't have gotten very far. Rob played the tape back in his mind and he couldn't remember seeing anyone in the area when he turned onto the block. Then it hit him, the kid he had seen on the corner. The more he thought about it, the more familiar the kid's face was. It finally dawned on him that it had been the kid he'd seen at Purple City with Diamonds. The fact that the upstart had made the first move infuriated Rob. He had warned his friend that they should've dealt with Diamonds immediately, but he wouldn't listen. Now Flames was gone. Rob vowed that his death wouldn't go unpunished. Diamonds had made the first move, but Rob would make the final move.

CHAPTER 10

Animal arrived at Purple City early the next morning. He hadn't slept all night and it showed by the bags under his eyes and his ruffled clothes. He was tired and weary, but more importantly, he was ready to take his leave of Miami.

He was met by the door by Unique. She was wearing a white tank top, black biker shorts and her roller skates. She skated up to him with a big grin on her face. "You look like shit." She joked.

Animal managed to muster a weak smile. "I feel like shit too. Where's the boss man?"

"He's in the back with the others. They're waiting for you."

Animal nodded and stepped into the club. At the same time, he was going through the curtain, G was on his way out. The two literally bumped into each other.

Standing in the brightly lit foyer Animal was able to get a good look at the man who called himself G. There was something about his dark skin and the structure of his face that tugged a cord of familiarity. Animal was about to apologize, but G spoke first.

"Watch where you're going, lil nigga." G bumped passed him.

Animal started to let it go, but he couldn't. "What the fuck is your problem, homie?" G had been spoiling for a fight since they'd met and Animal was more than willing to give him one.

"I ain't none of your fucking homie and my problem is you!" G told him.

"Blood, you've been acting like you're feeling some type of way about me ever since I got here. I ain't got a problem with you, but apparently you got one with me. Now we can keep grilling each other or go outside and beat the shit out of each other and get rid of this tension. What's popping?" Animal asked.

Anger flashed in G's eyes. His fist balled tightly and Animal tensed, anticipating the coming battle. G took a step towards Animal and stopped abruptly. Animal could see the conflicted look on G's face. With the tension between them had swelled to the point where it seemed like it would pop at any minute, G just sighed and shook his head.

"You don't get it, do you?" G asked.

"Get what?"

G motioned around. "All of it. Shorty, I seen a million cats like you come and go. Niggaz who think they're the hardest mutha fuckas on the planet until they run into somebody harder and your story ends with somebody consoling your mother and your homies pouring out liquor, telling war stories about how much of a good dude you were. "

Animal looked G up and down. "You think know me, nigga?"

"I know you better than you think I do, because I used to be you." G confessed. His eyes took on a far away look as if he was watching a movie in his head. "Yeah, I was out here putting in major work back in the days. My family was hood royalty and I was so eager to prove that I belonged. I was always the first one to bust my gun and the last one to leave the scene of the crime. I always said that when I went out, I wanted to go out like a gangster, all guns and glory. Well, God must've been listening because I got my wish." He pulled down the collar of his white t-shirt so Animal could see the scars that covered his entire chest and the side of his face. "You ever been hit with a shotgun at close range? Hurts like a mutha fucka, trust me on that. Getting shot up was painful, but not as painful as being abandoned. Of all the lives I saved that day, not a one of them after checked to see what happened to me. Not even my own family."

"But you lived." Animal pointed out.

G laughed as if the statement was the funniest he'd ever heard. "You call this living? I was a fucking ghetto star." He was emotional. "Now look at me. I'm a man without a face or a place in the world getting by as best I can by doing other people's dirty work."

Animal nodded. He felt like he understood G a little better. "I feel your pain, fam, but that still doesn't explain why you've been giving me a hard time."

"I swear each generation gets stupider than the last." G said in an irritated tone. "Dawg, we're damn near two sides of a mirror. You wanna know why I don't like you? Because in you I see everything that I used to be and could've been and what you're too stupid to try to be. Do you know what I would've given for a second chance they gave you? Of course, you don't, because if you did you'd still be down in Puerto Rico instead of up here trying to piss your life away."

"You don't understand. I got people I need to get home to." Animal told him.

G shook his head sadly. "You keep thinking them niggaz you wit is with you and you're gonna learn a hard lesson. Let's just hope than when somebody dumps as many bullets in you as they did in me, you're able to get up and walk away from it too."

"I hear you talking, Blood." Animal said.

"Don't hear me, *Blood*, listen to me. You think you're calling the shots, but you ain't nothing but a rat in a maze. Since you're content to do other people's dirty work, I got a message I want you to deliver to a cousin of mine when you get to New York. "

"I ain't no messenger, fam. Besides, New York is a big place and there's no guarantee me and your cousin will ever cross paths." Animal said.

"The fact that you've made it this far guarantees it. When that day comes, tell him that Auntie June's favorite nephew sends his regards and I'll see him soon." G said walked off, leaving Animal perplexed by his statement.

When Animal stepped into the main area of Purple City he saw Diamonds and his whole crew sitting at their usual table in the back. Minister was standing near the end of the table, eye ever vigilant. Diamonds sat flanked by Blue and Reign, throwing back shots. It was the middle of the day, but they were popping bottles and getting faded like it was Friday night.

When Diamonds saw Animal approaching, he stood up to embrace him. "Is that the illest nigga to ever fall

out of a bitch's twat? Gimmie some love, baby boy."
Diamonds hugged Animal. "Sit down, sit down. You're
the guest of honor at this lil celebration. Reign, why
don't you pour my man a taste."

Reign rolled her eyes. "Do I look like a fucking
waitress to you? Get one of those bitches to do it."

The smile faded from Diamonds' face. "You been
acting real fucking shitty for the past two days, Reign.
I don't know what the fuck your problem is, but you
better shake that shit and get with the program, *Ou
konprann?*" he switched to Creole, as he often did
when he was angry.

"Yeah, I understand." Reign got off and went to sit
over by the stage.

Diamonds watched her walk away and all he could
do was throw his hands up. "I don't know what it is
with these broads, man. One minute everything is

good, the next they're acting like the got sticks up their assess. You know what you mean, Animal?"

"Yeah, man." Animal told him. "So, you ready to fulfill your end?"

"Sure, sure, we gonna get to that. First, I wanna know all the details." Diamonds leaned in; anticipating the juicy story Animal had to tell.

Instead, Animal reached in his pocket and tossed a folded-up piece of cloth on the table. It flipped over on its side and Flames' tongue spilled out. "That enough detail for you?"

Blue jumped back with a start at the sight of the tongue. "What the fuck? Man, are you crazy or something, kid?"

"Nah, I ain't crazy. I'm just tired of bullshitting around. I got moves to make." Animal told him.

"That's the part I like about you most, Animal. You're always about your business first." Diamonds said. "Dig, me and Blue was talking this morning and we think our lil crew would be a lot stronger with a cat like you on the team. We making money hand over fist down here and I'll gladly break bread with you. What's up?"

"Diamonds, I'm flattered by your offer, but I can't accept it. My business in New York has already been too long neglected and I need to see to it." Animal said.

"I understand. Can't knock me for trying." Diamonds shook Animal's hand. "Minister will take you to the rental car that you're going to drive to New York. It's clean as a whistle. I rented it for a month using a dead man's credit card so by the time they get hip that the car ain't coming back, I trust you'll have handled your business and disposed of it."

"Bet. Now the name." Animal was anxious.

"Not here. The walls got ears." Diamonds stage whispered. "I wrote it on a piece of paper that Minister will give you before you depart." Diamonds saw that Animal was hesitant. "On the blood of my homie Buda, I wouldn't try to play you after what you done for me. Minister got your info."

Animal looked at Minister, who nodded. He didn't know Minister that well, but something about the man said that he was trustworthy. "A'ight, I'm out. Thanks for your help, fam."

"No problem, *mon ami*. We ain't come from the same woman, but this here," he placed his hand over his heart, "makes us brothers."

Animal followed Minister to the door. As he crossed the room he could feel Reign's eyes on him. He started to leave without saying anything, but he couldn't leave her hanging like that. "Well, I guess this is it." He approached her.

"I guess so. Have a safe trip." Reign said flatly.

Animal was silent for a few seconds. "Reign, I know you're still mad at me and I don't blame you, but I don't want us to part on bad terms."

"Ain't no us and ain't no terms. It ain't like we'll ever see each other again so let's just leave it as it is, a mistake. That's how you phrased it, wasn't it?"

"Reign…"

"Have a safe trip, Animal." She gave him her back.

Animal was going to press it, but that would most likely make it worse. He did feel terrible for the way things had gone down between he and Reign, but there was nothing he could do to change the past. His focus was on the future and his future was Gucci. He caught up with Minister, who was standing outside on the curb waiting for him. They were about to head to the car when Unique came skating out of Purple City.

Minister saw that the girl had something he wanted to say to Animal so he excused himself. "I'll get the car." He disappeared around the corner.

"You were just gonna leave without saying goodbye, huh?" Unique faked an attitude.

"My fault, ma. I'm just so excited to be going home." He told her.

"I've never been to New York, but I've heard a lot of stories about it. Maybe one day I'll come visit and you can give me the grand tour." Unique said.

"I'd love to, but honestly, I don't think I'll be there very long. Once my business is settled, I plan to take my lady and bounce." Animal said.

"She's lucky to have somebody like you." Unique told him.

Animal smiled at her. "I wish that were true. Sometimes it seems like I've brought more bad on her than good."

"I love we take the bad with the good. At least that's what I read somewhere."

"You're a wise young lady, Unique."

"Thanks." She said shyly. For a long moment she was quiet, looking down at her roller skates. She eventually looked up at Animal and her face had become serious. "Animal, I heard what my sister said to you. I hope she didn't hurt your feelings too bad."

Animal was surprised by the revelation. "Reign is your sister?"

"Yeah, everybody knows that, silly. You know with asses like ours, it's gotta be genetic." She twirled on her skates, giving Animal a full view of her. "Reign can come across like a cold bitch, but she's really a sweetheart once you get to know her. I think she really liked you and that's why she took it so hard when…you know."

Animal blushed. "Damn, did she tell you everything?"

Unique winked "We're sisters. Don't worry, your secret is safe with me. Anyway, I just wanted to say goodbye and wish you a safe trip." She wrapped her arms around his neck.

"Thanks, Unique. Take care of yourself." He squeezed her waist.

Something beyond Unique caught Animal's attention. A cluster of cars was coming through the intersection. It wasn't unusual at that time of the day, but something wasn't right. Animal scanned the cars and picked out a green Mercedes. Instead of the driver watching the road, his eyes were fixed on Animal and Unique. His danger alert was ringing like a fire alarm in the back of his head. Suddenly all the pieces fell into place. It was the same Mercedes he'd seen when he was leaving Flames' townhouse. By the time Animal reacted, a gun appeared in back window all hell broke loose.

The world moved in slow motion. Animal saw the bullets coming in his direction like thick droplets of water down a car's windshield. He spun, with Unique still in his arms, shielding her. The sound of her screams and shattering glass filled Animal's ears as the chaos erupted around him. Bullets whizzed past his head, riddling the front of Purple City and hitting several people that been unfortunate enough to be coming down that street. Animal shoved Unique to the ground and spun, holding the gun he had used to kill Flames, and returned fire.

"Die!" Animal screamed, firing at the Mercedes, and backing up for cover.

The driver's side window shattered and Rob temporarily lost control of the car, almost slamming into a cube truck that was coming from the opposite direction. Rob straightened the car out and floored the gas pedal. He was trying to escape, but too bad he didn't see Minister's car shoot out of the alley on the side of the club. The Lincoln slammed into the side of the Mercedes, pinning it against a parked car on the other side of the street thwarting Rob's great escape.

The shooter staggered from the backseat of the car. His face and clothes were bloody and his arm hung at a strange angle. Minister calmly walked up to him and put a bullet in his head. He moved to finish Rob off, but Animal stopped him.

"That one is for me." He walked up to the driver's side of the car, where Rob was pinned by the air bag.

Rob looked up at Animal and there was no fear in his eyes, only disgust that he had missed his target. Animal stuck the gun in Rob's ear and pulled the trigger twice. The airbag popped and Rob slumped over on his side. For good measure, Animal shot him twice more in the side.

There was a loud shriek that caused Animal to spin. When he looked to the club and saw the source of the noise, his heart sank. Reign knelt beside her sister, holding her still body in her arms. Unique's lifeless eyes stared vacantly into space but saw nothing.

Diamonds and Blue came storming out of Purple City, guns in hand and scanning the block. When Diamonds saw Reign kneeling over Unique, he looked like someone had just slapped him. He opened his mouth to speak, but no words came out. Unique had been like a little sister to Diamonds and seeing her bleeding out on the sidewalk sent him into shock.

"No." Animal whispered when he approached the scene. In the middle of Unique's tank top there was a small red spot that seemed to spread by the second. Animal had tried to save her, but once again he had been too little too late. "I am so sorry." He reached out to touch Unique's face and Reign spun on him.

"Don't you touch her!" she shouted with tear filled eyes.

"I tried to save her, Reign. I swear…"

"Don't." she stopped him. "They told me you were cursed. They said that whatever you touch dies, but I didn't listen. I just had to be next to you. Now you've brought death to my doorstep too. My poor, baby sister." She stroked Unique's face.

Everyone was twisted over what had happened to Unique, but Blue was the voice of reason. "I'm gonna call some of the boys and have them clean this shit up then call in a favor from downtown to see if we can get it swept under the rug to take some of the heat off us. Minister, get Animal out of here. If the police find him here when they show up, it's likely to mean a free trip the gas chamber for us all."

Animal didn't feel right about it. "Nah, I wanna stay and help. I wanna do something…anything. Just tell me what I can do?"

"I think you've done enough." Diamond said. He tossed Minister the keys to his truck. "Take this nigga to the rental car and then escort him to the highway. See to it that he leaves Miami immediately."

"I got you." Minister took Animal by the arm and steered him around the corner where Diamonds' truck was parked. He jumped behind the wheel and Animal climbed in on the passenger side. Minister fired the truck up and screeched out into traffic.

"Minister, I feel fucked up by just leaving her like that." Animal told him once they were away from Purple City.

"You'll feel worse if you're still around once Reign snaps out of it." Minister said seriously. "Unique is her baby sister and the only family she's got in the world. She blames you for this happening. A lot of niggaz in the hood got love and respect for Reign and will do just about anything for her, including putting your dick in the dirt. Right now, Reign is still in shock, but when the shock wears off it's in your best interest to be as far away from Miami as possible."

The two of them rode the rest of the way in silence. When they reached the airport, Minister pulled into the parking garage where the rental car was waiting. They jumped out of the car and Minister waited while Animal inspected the car and got situated. The Toyota wasn't much to look at, but it would get him to New York.

"The gas tank is full and if you look in the trunk you'll find the goodies Diamonds left for you." Minister told him.

"Thanks, Minister. Not just for the ride, but for everything else." Animal said.

"It's all good, brother. If we don't look out for each other, who will? I'll lead you to the highway and it's a straight shot up I-95 from there." Minister turned to walk away, but Animal stopped him.

"What about the name Diamonds promised me?"

"Right, I almost forgot." Minister reached into the pocket of his suit jacket and produced a small, folded piece of paper which he placed in Animal's hand. "Good luck to you, soldier." Minister shook Animal's hand and headed back to the truck.

Animal looked down at the small piece of paper in his hand. It seemed so small and unassuming, but it held the fate of someone's life and the answer to Animal's question in the folds. With trembling hands, Animal unfolded the small square. His breath caught in his chest when the mystery was finally solved. On it two names were written, with the role of each man scribbled next to it. One said *shooter* and the other said *bag man*. Animal couldn't believe his eyes. Both men knew him and both knew how he would react, but they figured with him being dead there would be no repercussions. They were wrong...*dead* wrong and he would show them as much.

Animal jumped behind the wheel of the rental car and the loud roar of the engine matched the roar of the beast deep within him. He shot out of the parking garage like a bat out of hell, leaving Minister in his rearview with a confused look on his face. He didn't need him to guide him to his destination. The names of those who had wronged him had been revealed and that was all the direction he needed. There was no place on earth where they could hide that would save them from his vengeance.

To be continued…

Made in United States
Orlando, FL
30 March 2022

16301850R00114